Protecting Alabama

Protecting Alabama

SEAL of Protection
Book 2

By Susan Stoker

Cover Design by Chris Mackey, AURA Design Group
Edited by Missy Borucki

Manufactured in the United States

Table of Contents

Chapter One

Age 2

"OUT! WANT OUT!"

"Shut *up* you stupid whore! I'll let you out when you shut up and not a second before! You hear me, brat?"

Alabama Ford Smith only cried harder. She didn't understand why Mama wouldn't let her out of the closet. She was hungry and it was dark and scary inside the small room.

"Maaaaamaaaaaa."

Alabama stopped and listened against the door and couldn't hear anything. Was Mama still there? Alabama tried to reach the doorknob, but her little, two-year-old fingers couldn't grasp it. The knob wouldn't turn anyway; it was locked from the outside.

After an hour of wailing and crying, Alabama laid down on the floor amongst the shoes, boxes, and musty smelling hats and gloves. She sniffed. Mama had been serious. Alabama wasn't going to get to come out of the little room until she shut up. She didn't know what a whore was, but it had to be a bad little girl like her. She would try harder to please Mama.

Age 6

"ALABAMA FORD, HOW many times do I have to tell you to shut the hell up? Too damn many. If I hear one more word out of you, you'll be sorry!"

"But Mama…"

"Dammit, I warned you…"

Alabama felt her mama's hand hit the side of her face right before she went sailing down the three stairs that led from the kitchen into the family room. She watched as Mama came at her with murder in her eyes. She couldn't quite dodge the foot that was aiming at her head. It glanced off of her and she could see that just made Mama madder. The next hit came from the same foot into her side. Alabama curled into the smallest ball she could and tried to protect her head. She knew she wasn't the smartest girl, but Alabama figured if she had any chance of being able to walk in the morning, she had to protect her knees as well. Mama loved to kick them and then laugh as she tried to hobble around the house.

"Stupid whore bitch. Why do you have to be so stupid? I *said* to shut up. I'll teach you to speak out of turn. Don't. Ever. Speak. Again. Unless. I. Ask. You. Something."

Spittle flew from Mama's mouth as she enunciated and kicked at Alabama with each word spoken. Alabama finally got it. She shut up. Even as a six year old, Alabama knew Mama was serious. Mama meant every word that came out of her mouth. That was the year Alabama stopped talking unless she was asked a direct question.

Age 11

"ALABAMA, DO YOU want to talk to the nice policeman?"

Alabama looked up at the stern looking officer. He was tall and muscular and looked so strong. She sniffed a little and tried to be brave. Mama had walloped her this morning with the skillet she'd been holding. Alabama knew it was her fault. She'd made the mistake of asking Mama when she'd be home later that day. She *knew* better. How many times had Mama told her never to talk to her? Too many. And Alabama asked anyway. She knew Mama had been aiming at her head, but Alabama turned at the last minute and the skillet collided with her arm instead. Over the course of the day it had turned a nasty shade of purple. Of course a teacher noticed and insisted on taking her to the principal's office.

The principal was a nice enough lady, but she had

no idea what Mama was like. No one did. Alabama was beginning to think Mama was crazy. It wasn't a nice thing to think about your own mama, but she couldn't think anything else. After eleven years of living with her, Alabama finally figured out that other little girls didn't have to worry about their mama's hitting them if they spoke out loud at home. They didn't have to worry about skillets coming at their heads if they so much as coughed too loud.

Alabama figured this was her chance. Maybe this officer would protect her. Policemen were supposed to protect people. She told him everything. How Mama would lock her in the closet when she went out. How she wasn't allowed to talk at home. How Mama hit her all the time with whatever was handy. Alabama spilled her guts to the police officer in the hopes he'd take her away and give her to a nice family, one with a nice mama. When he kneeled down in front of her, took her hands, and smiled at her, Alabama knew she could finally relax. This man would help her. He'd protect her.

Age 12

ALABAMA LISTENED TO the mutterings of the people around her. She lay on the bed with her eyes closed. She thought back to the day at school about a year ago. She felt as if she'd aged ten years since that time. Twelve was too young to have to deal with this.

"Did you hear what happened? That her mother did this to her?"

"No way! Holy crap. Do you think she's done it before?"

"Hell yes. Look at her, Betty. No one does this the first time. I bet she's been waling on this child for years. She can't go back. You know it, I know it. Hell, even her mom knows it. I think that's why she did it."

There was silence. Alabama couldn't fall back to sleep, even though it's what she wished with all her heart. She wished she wasn't there anymore. She'd trusted the police officer last year. He said it'd be okay. He said she wouldn't have to worry about her mama anymore. He lied. Seven days after she told the policeman everything, she was back at home. Mama didn't like it that she'd told. Apparently she'd gone through interviews with the police and Child Protective Services who were checking to make sure Mama was a good mama. Alabama knew Mama could be nice when she wanted to. Apparently she'd convinced everyone Alabama was a typical almost-teenager who was just rebelling. Mama told everyone she'd hit herself with the skillet in order to get attention. So Alabama was sent back.

Things got worse at home after that. Alabama learned never to say a word. She kept her mouth shut.

Mama was scary. Alabama learned she'd have to protect herself. No one else would do it for her.

Mama had finally lost it tonight. Alabama had been in her room with the door shut when she'd gotten home from the bars. Mama had burst into her room and started waling on her. Mama yelled such horrible things. She'd told Alabama she was a mistake—that Alabama never should've been born, that she wasn't wanted. Mama yelled how she'd even given Alabama the stupidest name she could think of; how Alabama was named after the state Mama had gotten pregnant in and even gave Alabama the middle name of the stupid car she'd been conceived in. Alabama hadn't even known that Smith wasn't Mama's last name. Mama made it up because she didn't want her baby to have *her* name.

Alabama remembered Mama leaving the room and coming back a moment later with the dreaded skillet. It wasn't until Alabama woke up in the ambulance she realized, based on what the EMTs were saying, that Mama had broken her jaw. Okay, Mama had broken most of Alabama's face too—nose, cheekbone, and even her eye socket had been cracked.

Lying in the hospital bed with her jaw wired shut, Alabama made a vow to her twelve year old self. No matter what happened in the future, Alabama would never trust anyone to protect her again. If her mama didn't want her, if the police couldn't or wouldn't protect her…who would? She was nobody. Alabama had a made up last name and a first name based on the state her mom had sex in.

Age 16

SIXTEEN YEAR OLD Alabama walked down the hall of the high school with her head down, clutching her books. Another birthday had passed with no one knowing. No one said "Happy Birthday," no one gave Alabama any presents. She was the "weird" kid in school. She never spoke to anyone. She kept her head down and didn't make trouble. She aced all her tests and loved English, but she refused to answer any questions in class. Alabama never talked to her class-mates. She went to school every day, minded her own business, and kept to herself. She didn't cause any trouble at school or at her foster home.

Alabama's foster mom tried to engage her, tried to get Alabama to open up, with no luck. Alabama had learned her lesson. She spoke only when spoken to and only when absolutely necessary. She got a job at the local library stocking shelves. Alabama saved her money for the day she'd turn eighteen and would move out on her own. She'd never rely on anyone again. Alabama was on her own.

Chapter Two

CHRISTOPHER "ABE" POWERS looked around the room and sighed. It was time to break it off with Adelaide. After dating her for about three months, Abe realized he didn't really even like her all that much. He supposed he'd stayed with Adelaide this long because she was good in bed, and he was lazy. The hunt for women had gotten old. It was all just a game. Abe knew he was good looking. He wasn't conceited, but he'd had his share of women over the years...too many, truth be told.

Abe was a Navy SEAL. He was used to women hearing that term and practically begging to go home with him. He'd seen how his buddy Matthew, also known as Wolf, had settled down with the love of his life. Caroline was different from almost every woman Abe had ever met. She was smart and pretty, even if she didn't think of herself that way, and stronger than he would've guessed. She also hated Adelaide. He supposed he should've listened to Caroline when she'd tried to tell him Adelaide wasn't good enough for him, but he'd enjoyed the things Adelaide could do with her tongue too much to call it off.

Abe met Caroline on an airplane, of all things. In fact, she'd saved his life, along with everyone else's on the plane. If it wasn't for Caroline's chemist background, they all would've been drugged and the terrorists would have killed everyone on the plane for their own agenda. Caroline and Wolf had been through hell, but they'd come out all right on the other side.

Abe thought about Wolf and Ice. They hadn't had an easy time of it, that's for sure. Surviving the terrorist hijacking was just the tip of the iceberg. The SEAL team had just returned from a mission and learned that Caroline had been taken into Federal custody after an attempt on her life. The team had joined her protection detail, but the terrorists had found her again. They'd taken Caroline captive and tortured and beaten her trying to find out how she'd figured out the terrorist plot on the airplane. The team had to actually rescue her from the ocean after the terrorists had thrown her overboard with weights tied around her ankles.

It had been a sobering time for the team, knowing how much Wolf loved Caroline and how they'd all felt helpless watching her be tortured and almost killed.

While Abe wanted a relationship like Caroline and Wolf had, he definitely didn't want his woman to have to go through the hell Caroline lived through. Abe didn't think he'd be able to stand it. He hated to see women and children hurt—they should be protected by any means necessary.

He supposed that was why he was a SEAL. Abe wanted to join the military and serve his country, but it wasn't until basic training and seeing the SEALs in training that he decided he wanted to be one of the best of the best.

Abe's team *was* one of the best. The team had been on too many missions to count and while they weren't fun, the missions were certainly necessary.

Abe met Adelaide while out at *Aces Bar and Grill*, their usual hangout, after a mission one night.

He and Wolf and Mozart and the other guys had gotten hammered. Abe supposed it was partly because his friends were with him, but he'd taken Adelaide up on her proposition and gone home with her. He'd refused to take her girlfriend as well. Some of the other guys enjoyed that sort of thing, but Abe was a one-woman-at-a-time man. He always had been and always would be. He knew it was partly because of his father, but he'd never analyzed it.

Abe and Adelaide spent most of the night in bed. She'd been willing to try just about anything, and at the time, it'd been just what he was looking for. He needed to blow off steam and having sex, lots of it, was a great way to do that.

But now, he was realizing, Adelaide was a total bitch. He hated to compare every woman he met to Caroline, but he couldn't help it. He was standing there listening to Adelaide gossip with her coworkers and wishing he was anywhere else. How had he stooped this low? This wasn't like him at all.

"Can you believe she brought *that*?"

"I know, ridiculous!"

"I guess she can't cook at all. But seriously, why didn't she cater something?"

Abe sighed loudly. Shit. Why did Adelaide and her catty coworkers even care that someone apparently brought a bowl full of vegetables instead of making a dish or bringing something catered to the pot luck? Jesus. Didn't they have anything better to do?

"Adelaide, I'm going to head over and grab something to eat. Do you want anything?" Abe might be ready to ditch her, but he'd treat Adelaide right in the meantime. It was hard wired into Abe's very being. He'd never disrespect Adelaide by breaking up with her in front of her friends and coworkers, but it was coming…and soon.

"No, but thanks, sweetie, you know I'm watching my weight." Adelaide snuggled up and leaned into him, making sure to brush her breasts against his arm. "I'll show you what I *want* later. Hurry back, I'll be waiting for you."

Abe shrugged out of her hold and managed to escape without having to endure being kissed. He eyed the lipstick she'd caked on her mouth earlier that night with disgust. Didn't she know how horrible that stuff tasted? Not to mention how Abe hated having it smeared all over his lips when Adelaide kissed him. He suspected she did it on purpose, a kind of ownership thing on her part. He snorted. *He* was supposed to be the dominant in the relationship, but Adelaide took the word to a whole new level. The more Abe thought about it the more he realized she didn't care about *him* per se, he could be anyone. Adelaide only cared that Abe was a SEAL and good looking. Yup, it was definitely time to break it off.

Abe walked over to the overflowing food table. Adelaide's company was having their annual banquet to thank their employees for a job well done over the past year. Wolfe Family Realty was the top realty company in their small town of Riverton and Adelaide was one of the most successful realtors they had. Abe supposed Adelaide had a teensy right to be entitled, but it wasn't enough for him to want to stay with her.

The Wolfe Family had been in the real estate business for years. They tried to keep their company close-knit, but it was obviously more of a wish than an actual fact. Abe had lived in Riverton a long time and didn't know most of the people at the event.

Abe grabbed a plate and got in the short line of people waiting to make their way down the line of delicious looking food. Abe took a step backward to avoid being run into by a man not paying attention where he was walking, and stepped on the foot of the person standing in line behind him.

Turning around Abe apologized, "I'm so sorry. Are you all right?"

Getting a good look at the woman who he'd stepped on made him forget what it was he was saying.

The woman was gorgeous. Abe didn't think she'd even tried to fancy herself up for the event, and that just made her stand out more. She came up to about his chin and had brown shoulder length hair, pulled back away from her face by a headband, but wisps of hair had escaped the wide swath of leather to frame her face. Abe thought she looked like she was wearing a bit of makeup—mostly around her eyes, and her lips were shiny with what looked like gloss. The lack of lipstick was a huge turn on for him, especially considering Adelaide's penchant for caking it on.

Abe continued his perusal of the fascinating woman standing behind him. She was wearing a pair of jeans with a top that had some ruffles on the sleeves. It was cut low in front, but not so low to be provocative—sexy because it left what was there mostly to the imagination.

Abe could see only a hint of her curves. She was wearing a pair of flip-flops with flowers on the band and her toenails were painted a pale pink. Everything about her had Abe's complete attention.

Abe suddenly realized he'd asked her a question, but she hadn't answered. He tried to look her in the eyes, but she was looking at the ground. He could see the faint blush on her cheeks. God, blushing? When was the last time he'd seen a woman blush? The Alpha male inside him stood up and took notice. She was obviously shy and that made her even more endearing.

Abe repeated himself as they shuffled forward in the line. "I'm really sorry. Did I hurt you with my big feet?" He willed her to look up at him.

The fascinating woman just shook her head and refused to look up.

"Hey, if you don't look at me I'll think you're lying to try to spare my feelings," he teased, hoping he'd get to see the color of her eyes.

"I'm fine," she said in a voice so low he almost didn't hear her.

Her voice was raspy, as if she hadn't used it in a long while and the low tone just made it sexier. The sound of it went through Abe and settled in his heart. Amazingly, he felt the hair on his arms stand up on end. Whoa.

Abe scrunched down and tried to look her in the eyes. She gave him a small chin lift as if to say, *"look."*

Abe turned and saw the line had moved forward and it was his turn to shuffle down the food table. He grabbed a plate and turned to the mysterious woman and held it out to her. Abe finally got to see her eyes when she looked up at him in confusion. Her eyes were a pale gray with streaks of blue. He figured in a different light they'd probably look more blue than gray. To answer her unasked question, Abe told her while waggling the plate, "For you."

Abe watched as she took the plate gingerly, as if it was a bomb he'd offered her instead of a simple dish. Abe took one off the top of the stack for himself and tried to engage the woman as he walked through the food line.

"What's good? What did you bring?" When she didn't answer, but concentrated instead on serving herself, Abe tried to joke with her. "Let me guess, which one is yours...hmmm, the homemade rolls? No? What about the macaroni salad there? Oh, I know... the lame bowl of vegetables?"

Realization dawned about the same time she bit her lip and looked away from the table in consternation. Oh shit.

"Ah fuck, I'm sorry. I didn't mean anything by that."

When she didn't say anything but only shrugged and continued to look as if she wanted to be anywhere but standing next to him, Abe tried desperately to backpedal.

"Seriously, I'm sorry. That was beyond rude. Jesus. You must think I'm the biggest asshole. I love veggies."

When she still didn't say anything, Abe transferred his plate to one hand, grasped her elbow lightly with the other, and pulled her away. They'd both filled their plates and had reached the end of the table. "Look at me."

At the commanding tone in Abe's voice, she looked up, finally.

Abe tamped down his feeling of triumph at her reaction to his demand. God, now wasn't the time for his Alpha side to come out, but deep down he reveled in her continued reactions to his words.

"I'm sorry. Okay?"

"Okay," she again said in a soft voice, nodding at the same time to reinforce her answer.

Loving the sound of her voice, even if he'd only heard her say a few words, Abe firmly stated, "Look, that's more than I brought. I'm being a mooch. At least *you* contributed." The hesitant smile that crept across her face was worth any embarrassment Abe felt at putting his foot in his mouth.

"I can't cook. Believe me, it's better I brought vegetables than if I tried to actually make something," she admitted sheepishly, again speaking to him in her soft husky way.

Somehow knowing her speaking to him was a victory of some sort, but not knowing exactly why, Abe gave her a huge grin.

Still holding his plate in one hand, Abe held out his other hand and said, "I'm Christopher. My friends call me Abe, but you can call me Christopher."

"Alabama." The woman replied politely, but didn't reach for his hand to shake and didn't ask any questions about his name, or nickname. Alabama was gripping her plate with both hands as if her life depended on it. It didn't faze Abe though. Trying to keep the conversation going, Abe simply nodded at her and said, "It's very nice to meet you, Alabama. I guess you work here too?" He watched as her face lost all animation and her eyes darted away from his, as if looking for something to distract her. Alabama's teeth came out to nibble at her lower lip. Abe knew she was going to bolt right before she spoke.

"I gotta go."

Alabama didn't even apologize or try to change the subject. She literally just fled away from him.

Abe watched her go. He had no idea what it was about her, but he knew he wanted to get to know Alabama more than anything he'd wanted in his life recently. There was something about her that made all of his protective instincts come flying to the surface. There was a story there, and he wanted to know it. Abe wanted to know all about Alabama.

Chapter Three

ALABAMA FLINCHED AS she scurried away from the hottest guy she'd ever seen. If her hands were free and she could've smacked herself in the forehead, she would have. God. She was *such* a dork. Seriously. Alabama didn't think she'd ever been so mortified in her life. Ok, she *knew* she'd never been so embarrassed before. Probably because she always avoided people and never tried to engage them in conversation.

Christopher. *Christopher.* Not Chris, but Christopher. His name was even hot. Alabama didn't know what his last name was, but she was sure it was something equally cool. She didn't like the sound of "Abe" at all. He didn't look like an "Abe"—even if that was what his friends called him, Alabama knew she never would.

She hadn't meant to really engage him in conversation; it went against every instinct she had. Alabama wasn't a talker. She wasn't ever going to be a talker. She'd gotten better as she'd gotten older, but when Christopher said he was sorry so sweetly and contritely,

Alabama couldn't stop herself from trying to make him feel better. *She* was trying to make *him* feel better. Crazy. And when Christopher demanded in *that* voice for her to look at him, she couldn't help herself.

All her life, Alabama tried to please people—Mama, teachers, foster parents…but it never did any good. No one had ever been happy with Alabama. She spoke too much, she didn't talk enough, she was weird, she wasn't engaging enough…why couldn't Alabama stop trying to make others happy now? You'd think she'd have learned her lesson by now.

Alabama scooted over to the corner of the room and sagged into a chair, put her plate on her lap, and tried to regain her composure. What time was it? Could she leave yet? Yes, she was invited to the party by the Wolfe's, Alabama *did* work there after all, but she wasn't a realtor. She was a janitor. She cleaned the offices after everyone else had gone home. It wasn't glamorous, but she did it well. Alabama took pride in making sure everything was spotless. She actually liked the job because she didn't have to talk to anyone. She could put in her iPod and jam out to her favorite music as she cleaned.

Alabama knew every nook and cranny of the office. She probably knew more about what went on there than even the Wolfe's did. It was amazing what people would throw away, thinking that once it was in the trash it was "gone." She'd seen used condoms, antacids, sticky notes with love poems on them, and she'd even had to empty a trash can full of vomit. Alabama shook her head. If only they all knew what she had to deal with in cleaning the office.

Alabama knew most of the relators didn't even know she existed, and that was all right with her. She'd never made friends easily. Oh, she figured she was a nice enough person, she just wasn't very social. Alabama didn't enjoy idle chitchat and most women thought she was strange. Besides, making friends meant opening up and making herself vulnerable. Alabama tried one year after she'd moved to Riverton. There was another janitor who Alabama *thought* she'd befriended.

They'd been out to dinner a few times and spent some time together at work. Alabama had even started picking her up for their shift and driving her home as well. One night, Alabama overheard her talking on the phone to someone about what she really thought about their friendship. She'd only been using Alabama for the rides so she could save money. She'd told whoever was on the phone she thought Alabama was weird and she was glad she'd be getting her car back the next week. That was the last time Alabama had offered to drive her to and from work and the last time she'd tried to make friends.

Coming back to the present, Alabama looked at Adelaide across the room. She wished Adelaide didn't know she existed. The woman hadn't liked Alabama on sight. Alabama had no idea why. She'd been in the office, cleaning as usual, when Adelaide had come in late one night. They were both surprised to see each other, but Adelaide had ordered her out of her office and shut the door. Adelaide was in there for about thirty minutes before exiting again and telling Alabama she didn't need to clean her office that night.

Alabama just shrugged and continued on with her cleaning. That was it. Ever since that night, Adelaide shot daggers out her eyes every time she'd seen Alabama. Alabama had no idea what Adelaide hid in the office that night, but obviously it'd been something she didn't want anyone to know about. Alabama thought about searching the office and seeing what she could find, but she didn't bother. She honestly didn't really care. Whatever it was would only cause more trouble for her, she was sure of it.

Alabama had heard Adelaide's snide comments about her veggies before she'd gone to get in line. She knew that was where Christopher had heard about them, but she tried not to hold it against him. He'd been trying to joke with her, not be mean, and had no idea she'd brought them.

Alabama nibbled on the food she'd put on her plate unenthusiastically and watched the people all around her. There were, as usual, too many people in the small space, but the Wolfe's didn't want to hear about having their annual "get together" anywhere else. It was tradition to have it in their business space, so that was where it was going to be, period. Most of the people were laughing and talking easily. The volume was loud in the room because of the size of the crowd. But at least everyone seemed happy and relaxed.

Alabama watched as Christopher made his way back to Adelaide's side. It really was too bad he was with her. Adelaide certainly didn't deserve Christopher. Alabama remembered back to when he'd handed her a plate. He'd done it so nonchalantly, as if he did that sort of thing all the time, and he probably did. It seemed to be ingrained in him to take care of others, but, she couldn't help but think, who took care of him? Adelaide certainly didn't. She didn't even notice that when she grabbed his arm when he came up beside her again, it jostled his hand and punch spilled over the edge of the cup to land on his shirt. Adelaide didn't even look up from the conversation she was having to notice his scowl or to help him mop up the spilled drink.

Even with her actions, Alabama noticed that Christopher continued to watch out for Adelaide. Alabama watched as he pulled her out of the way of two men who were trying to get past the group of women and how he took the empty glass out of her hand when she was done with it. Adelaide ignored him and hadn't even thanked him. Alabama could watch and appreciate Christopher's actions, but she had no idea how it actually felt to be treated that way.

Did Adelaide even recognize how much Christopher did for her? Did she realize how he protected her in so many little ways? Alabama tried to put herself in Adelaide's shoes; if Christopher was her boyfriend would she take advantage of the things he'd do for her? She mentally shrugged. She'd never had anyone in her entire life bother to look out for her so she couldn't imagine what she'd do. Whatever. Alabama didn't need anyone. She got along just fine by herself, at least that was what she tried to tell herself.

Alabama was so engrossed in covertly watching Christopher with Adelaide she missed the first sign of alarm. It wasn't until she saw Christopher actually drop the plate he was holding, ignore the food splattering all over their legs, and grab Adelaide by the arm, that she realized something might be wrong.

Alabama looked over toward the buffet table and saw that the table, and the curtain behind it, was on fire, and the fire was spreading fast. The room, which was overfull to begin with, was quickly filling with smoke and she could hear people screaming in panic. Alabama quickly dropped her own, now almost empty, plate and looked around at her exit options.

Ever since she was young and needed to try to escape Mama when she was pissed, Alabama made sure to make note of where the exits were in whatever situation she was in. That knowledge had saved Alabama from a beating more than once in her life and now it might just save her life.

Most of the people were heading toward the front door, the same door they'd entered earlier in the night. It was human nature to head for the door you knew about rather than trying to find an alternative exit.

Alabama knew there was a side door, but it was in the opposite direction from where most of the people in the room were trying to get out and it was down a short hall off the main room. It couldn't be seen from the main area where the party was taking place and thus it wasn't even an option for the panicking crowd. The smoke was billowing up from the curtains and was black and heavy. Alabama could feel the air thinning and it was becoming harder and harder to breathe.

Alabama had actually taken two steps toward the hall, and freedom, when she stopped. She thought about all the people who most likely wouldn't be able to get out the other exit because of the crowd of panicked partygoers. They'd surely block the door once they lost air. She'd seen enough news footage of crowded bars and nightclubs that had caught fire and the resulting carnage resulting in the press of people trying to get out a blocked door. If everyone continued to push and shove and try to get out the main door, it would soon be unpassable. Christopher wouldn't be able to get out.

Before she'd even made the conscious thought to move, Alabama was headed toward where she'd last seen Christopher. She quickly realized she wouldn't be able to stay upright if she wanted to breathe. Alabama dropped to her knees and started crawling as fast as she could. Thank God she was wearing pants. Alabama headed to the other side of the room, away from the freedom the side exit offered, but toward Christopher. He'd never been in this building and would have no idea about that other door. Somehow Alabama also knew he wouldn't leave Adelaide and the other women he'd been standing near. Christopher would do what he could to get them out.

Alabama lost precious minutes trying to get her bearings in the room, which seemed so much bigger when she couldn't see and when it was filled with smoke. She coughed once, then coughed again. She tried to hurry. Alabama knew time was running out. Finally, she reached the place where Christopher had been standing with Adelaide—they weren't there, but she saw a group of people huddled against the wall nearby.

Alabama scurried over to them but grabbed the arm of the man she passed along her way. She pointed toward the other side of the room where the hallway was and said urgently, "There's another door. Through the hall—over there… Go!"

The man didn't hesitate; he simply grabbed the hand of the woman next to him and left to go to where Alabama had pointed. They disappeared into the smoke filled room in a matter of seconds. If Alabama hadn't touched him she would've wondered if she'd dreamed him. She continued along the wall looking for Christopher and steered anyone she met along the way toward the other side of the room. They all looked thankful for her assistance, but none encouraged her to come with them. They just turned around and headed where she'd pointed.

After pointing the way out to several groups of people, she finally reached Christopher and Adelaide. They were on their knees huddled against the wall. Christopher had taken off his sports coat and put it around Adelaide. He'd also taken off his white dress shirt and tied it around Adelaide's head to try to help her breathe more easily. He'd tucked Adelaide into his front and was hovered over her protectively. Alabama could see him trying to take in the room, most likely to find an escape.

Alabama took half a second to admire Christopher's physique before snapping herself back to the emergency at hand. She didn't have time to gawk at how muscular he was and ignored how her stomach actually clenched at her first view of Christopher's six pack abs.

"Christopher," Alabama yelled as she grabbed his bicep, feeling it bulge under her fingertips. "There's another door over there." She pointed toward the other side of the room and the hallway that she'd been directing people to.

Expecting him to immediately snatch Adelaide up and head for safety, Alabama was surprised when he ignored her words and instead gripped her arm urgently. "Are you okay, Alabama?"

While she loved that he'd asked about her, now wasn't the time. They had to get out of there. It was getting hard to talk and hear anything with the noise of the fire.

Alabama simply nodded. "The door is that way." She pointed again and tried again to get him to go.

"Are you sure?" Christopher asked—his voice gritty with the smoke he'd inhaled.

Alabama nodded urgently. Crap, if he wouldn't go on his own, she'd have to make him. "Follow me," she ordered.

They turned to crawl across the floor but Adelaide refused to budge.

"Where are you going? No! The door is here, we have to stay here. It'll clear in a second." Adelaide started harshly coughing—her voice muffled from the shirt Christopher had wrapped around her.

Christopher turned back to Adelaide and spoke harshly to her. He was trying to convince her to go toward the other exit. Alabama could see the embers from the walls and other flammable material floating down and landing on Christopher's bare back as he kneeled next to and over Adelaide. He wasn't wearing a shirt and he was going to get burned if he crawled all the way across the room like that.

Alabama looked around desperately and spied a discarded suit coat lying on the ground, obviously thrown off in the panic of the other people. She scrambled over to it and grabbed a pitcher of water still sitting forlornly on a festive tablecloth. She walked on her knees back to Christopher and without warning, dumped the water over his head and watched it cascade over his hair and down his back.

She felt badly for just a moment, but then decided it was better he be pissed at her than be burned. Ignoring Adelaide's shrieks of outrage at her actions, Alabama thrust the jacket she'd pilfered off the floor at Christopher.

"To protect your back." She watched as Christopher didn't even quibble or say anything about the way she'd drenched him and shrugged on the jacket. It was a tight fit, and not only because he was now wet. He was obviously much broader and muscular than the man who'd discarded the jacket. Christopher simply nodded at her then slicked back his now dripping hair. He turned back to Adelaide.

Having grown tired of her tirade, Christopher grasped Adelaide's upper arm tightly and simply demanded in that no nonsense voice of his, "Move."

Seeing he was serious, and finally deciding moving was the better course of action than just kneeling against a wall inside a burning room, Adelaide finally stopped her bitching and meekly nodded. Christopher dropped his hand from Adelaide's arm and gestured for Alabama to lead the way. Alabama did without any hesitation. She could feel Christopher right at her side. He hadn't just allowed Alabama to take the lead, he was right there next to her, as they moved across the room to the exit, but not letting her get out of his reach. His shoulder would every now and then brush against her butt, he was that close.

The room was scary now. It was loud. Really loud. And it was dark. Alabama knew the air in the room was almost depleted. All thoughts of how hot Christopher looked without a shirt on and how nice he'd been to her were now gone from her head. Alabama was concentrating solely on getting out of the building which was burning down with them still inside it.

Alabama was coughing nonstop and could feel Christopher jerking against her, coughing as well. As they crawled, Alabama's hand touched a piece of cloth on the ground. Without thinking she snatched it up and kept going. She reached back briefly and pressed it to Christopher's arm. He grabbed it and she hoped he was using it as a filter to breathe through, as she intended it to be. Alabama might not be thinking about how good-looking the man was, but that didn't mean she hadn't stopped worrying about him. Christopher needed to cover his face so he wouldn't inhale any more smoke then he already had. She didn't even think about herself. Alabama only wanted to protect Christopher.

As Alabama and Christopher crawled, they came across a few other people seemingly lost in the confusion and Alabama grabbed on to them and urged them to crawl along with them. By the time the group made it to the hallway and then to the door, they were a group of about ten people, all in one long line. Alabama stopped and pushed on the door. She panicked for just a second when it didn't budge, but Christopher came up beside her and put his strength to it alongside hers. Their combined weight made it spring open. Fresh air swept into her face and Alabama took a deep breath.

The fresh air felt great, but the influx of oxygen into the hallway and toward the burning room just seemed to piss the fire off. Black smoke rolled out the door and the motley crew which had crawled across the fiery hell didn't waste any time getting out. One by one, they crawled through the door, got to their feet, and ran away from the burning building as fast as they could.

Alabama sat next to the door and helped everyone get out. She steadied them as they crawled out the door and tried to stand up. She couldn't stop coughing, but then again, neither could anyone else. Deep hacking coughs echoed in the air around them. If the fire hadn't been raging around them, all she would've heard was people coughing. As it was, she barely heard herself, nevertheless everyone else. She saw Christopher hesitate before he left, but Adelaide latched on to his arm, pulled him away and he disappeared out into the clean air.

Looking inside one more time after the last person in their group crawled out, Alabama didn't see anyone else. The fire was licking the ceiling and it was hot. Hotter than anything she'd ever experienced before. If anyone else was still inside, she didn't think there was any way they'd survive.

Alabama hadn't had time to think before, but what she'd just done scared the hell out of her and she started shaking. It was okay. She was okay. She'd gotten Christopher out. She'd gotten others out. Thank God, she knew about this exit.

Finally stumbling away from the door, Alabama looked around at the total chaos that was around her. There were fire trucks pulling up at the curb and people sitting and standing around the building in shock. She saw some news trucks driving in as well. This would be a huge story, she knew.

Alabama continued to cough, but ignored it as she frantically looked around. Finally seeing Christopher with Adelaide made her tense muscles relax a fraction. He was here. He was safe. Why that meant so much to her, she couldn't say. Hell, she didn't even know the man. There was just something about how Christopher talked with her as if he was interested and how he'd treated Adelaide that struck a chord within Alabama.

Something deep inside her that had hoped and prayed for someone to take her side, to protect her from Mama, sat up and took notice of Christopher. He was the kind of man she wanted. He was the kind of man that would look after his woman. Christopher would never let anyone hurt her. She knew firsthand that kind of man didn't come along every day. Even though he wasn't hers, she knew the world was a better place because he was in it.

She watched as Adelaide buried her face against Christopher's throat and wailed. Nastily, Alabama thought if Adelaide had the energy and ability to cry that hard and not cough up a lung, Adelaide was in better shape than most of the people sitting around her, including Christopher. Adelaide should've been more interested in how Christopher was than losing her shit.

Alabama watched as Christopher tried to comfort the woman in his arms while attempting to catch his own breath at the same time.

Alabama noticed two EMTs making their way through the people sitting haphazardly around on the grass trying to ascertain who needed help first. Everyone was coughing, but for the most part most people seemed to be all right. When one of the men made his way over to her she quietly and succinctly spoke her concerns to him, while brushing off his questions about her own well-being.

Finally understanding what she wanted, she watched as the EMT left and walked over to Christopher. Seeing he was going to be treated sooner rather than later, Alabama turned her attention toward getting out of there and back to her small apartment. It was a piece of crap, but it was home, and she desperately wanted to go home.

Alabama would figure out what was going on with her job later. The cleaning crew would be the last thing the Wolfe's would be concerned about right now. She'd wait a bit before contacting them to see what her next steps needed to be. She *needed* that job, but she didn't want to be selfish when others were hurt and everyone would be concerned about their jobs and livelihoods.

Alabama didn't look back toward the man she wished was hers. She simply walked away from the chaotic scene. There was no use wishing for something that would never happen. It was what it was. She'd learned her lesson a long time ago. Alabama had to be satisfied with their brief encounter and that Christopher was being cared for.

Abe looked up at the EMT that came toward them. Thank god, the EMT could take over caring for Adelaide and he could get the hell out of there. Abe wanted to find Alabama and thank her. He was surprised when the guy spoke to him specifically and didn't even look at the semi-hysterical woman trying to bury herself in his arms.

"Sir? I've been told you were burned? I'd like to take a look and make sure it's just superficial."

"Burned?" Abe was confused. Who said he was burned? Was he hurt and just didn't realize it?

"Turn around, sir, let's get this coat off and see how bad it is."

Abe coughed and let go of Adelaide who was cutting off the circulation in his arm. She resisted, but the EMT firmly instructed her to let go so he could check his back. The coat burned a bit as it slid off his back, but Abe showed no outward sign of discomfort. As far as pain went, it was low, especially compared to some of the injuries he'd received on his missions.

"Okay, it doesn't look too bad, sir," the EMT said briskly. "It looks like some of the embers landed on your back while you were getting out of there. I'm assuming you didn't have this jacket on the entire time? It's a good thing you put your coat back on, that's for sure. You would've been burned a lot worse if you hadn't. Look at the back of this."

Abe looked at the jacket the man held out and was amazed. He hadn't felt anything hitting his back while he'd been against the wall with Adelaide, adrenaline he supposed. But if Alabama hadn't had the presence of mind to douse him with water and to give him that coat…Alabama! Where was she? All of a sudden he desperately wanted to find her, to make sure she was all right, to thank her, hell…for all sorts of reasons he didn't understand.

Abe looked around and didn't see her anywhere. Did she get out?

"Who did you say told you to check me out?" Abe knew the man hadn't said, but it had to have been Alabama, no one else would have known he'd been burned. He needed to make sure.

"The lady over there…" The EMT pointed where he'd last seen Alabama and she wasn't there. "Well, she *was* over there. She was wearing jeans and wasn't very tall."

Abe nodded, a little irritated at his less-than-flattering description of the woman he found fascinating and gorgeous. "I know who it was. Thanks, man."

Abe didn't notice the snarl on Adelaide's face as he confirmed Alabama's presence.

SUSAN STOKER

"You know she's a janitor right?" Adelaide said malevolently, making herself known for the first time since the EMT had joined them. "She's weird and cleans toilets for a living."

"*You* know she just saved your life right?" Abe said without missing a beat. "Hell, she saved a *lot* of lives today, including mine. I don't care if she's an escaped felon or the queen of fucking England."

Adelaide just turned her head away and coughed dramatically.

"Come on, let's go and clean off your back, then you'll be good to go," the EMT said uncomfortably, not liking being in the middle of their disagreement.

Abe wanted nothing more than to leave Adelaide sitting on the ground, but he couldn't. It wouldn't be right, no matter how upset he was over the whole situation. He helped her up and put his arm around her waist and assisted her to the back of one of the ambulances that was lined up at the curb.

Feeling Adelaide's thin waist did nothing for Abe anymore. He couldn't even believe he used to think she was sexy. When he'd first seen her at *Aces* in her little black dress he'd been infatuated. She'd seemed like the perfect woman. Now he knew better. She was mean, and mean trumped looks every day of the week.

Knowing this wasn't really the place; he couldn't, and wouldn't, wait any longer.

"Adelaide, this isn't how I wanted to do this, but it's

time we moved on. We had a good time together, but I don't see us going anywhere."

"You're dumping me?" Adelaide shrieked not even coughing. Obviously Abe's shirt had adequately protected her while they were in the fiery hell. "What the hell? I thought you were this great protector, this great Alpha male. But when I'm at my lowest and hurt you're telling me we're over? Are you dumping me for the *janitor*?"

When he didn't say anything but only stared at her with derision, she sneered, "You prick. You'll regret this."

"I already do." Abe walked away shaking his head. He'd never understand women. Never. Walking away, he was already making plans in his head on how to find Alabama. She didn't know it yet, but she'd be seeing him again very soon. He'd contact Tex if he had to. Tex could find anyone. Tex used to be on a SEAL team, but after losing his leg on a mission he'd moved to Virginia and started his own independent private investigator business.

Tex was still close to all of the team and he'd helped locate Caroline when she'd been kidnapped by terrorists earlier that year. Tex would help him find Alabama, and then Abe could get to work seriously getting to know her.

Abe hadn't been this excited to get to know a woman in a long time; too long. He couldn't wait. Alabama wouldn't know what hit her. She'd be his.

Chapter Four

ALABAMA COUGHED AND watched the news the next night sadly. The anchorman was covering the fire. Apparently one of the cords to a crock pot on the buffet table shorted out and caught the cheap paper tablecloth on fire. Alabama couldn't help the mean thought that at least her veggies didn't burn the place down; it was someone's fancy catered food they'd brought.

By the time someone noticed, the small flame had spread and the curtains were already on fire. Luckily no one was killed, but there were still about a dozen people in the hospital. They were being treated for smoke inhalation and burns. Too many people were trapped trying to shove out the door. The news people had interviewed a few bystanders standing around. Most had said how scared they were and how they thought they were going to die.

Alabama recognized one couple who she'd pointed towards the hall and the door. They'd talked about how the room was dark and scary and even mentioned how someone had pointed them toward the side door so they could get out. They had no idea who it was though. The person interviewing them seemed interested at first, but then someone was wheeled by on a gurney, and apparently that was more interesting than the unhurt bystanders.

A part of Alabama was glad. She had no interest in being interviewed or pointed out. Anyone would have done what she'd done. At least she thought they would. She hated being in the spotlight. But another part of her was a little hurt. If someone had saved *her* life, she sure as hell would've made sure she noticed who it was and at the very least thanked them. Oh well.

Alabama's lungs still hurt, but she honestly couldn't complain, she was here and alive, *and* she'd helped many others get out. She hadn't bothered to go to the hospital. Once she saw Christopher was being seen for the burns on his back, she'd just left. Cleaning offices for a living didn't give her a lot of extra money, and Alabama figured a trip to the hospital and paying a co-pay for a doctor to tell her she was fine wasn't a good way to spend her hard-earned money.

She snuggled down into the blanket on her couch. The little apartment was all Alabama could afford on her salary. She was saving up her money for a down payment for a house of her own. She didn't know what house, or where, but she'd do whatever she could to have her very own space. Growing up the way she did made her crave a place of her very own. Her own safe place. Even though she'd made the apartment as cozy as she could, Alabama would never feel safe until she had her own house and her own space.

Her foster homes had never felt safe. Alabama always had to be careful of the other foster kids and even sometimes the parents. Lord knew she never felt safe with her mama. Her current apartment was perfect for now; it was small and cheap and allowed her to save money each month.

Alabama was proud of the amount of money she'd been able to save so far. She was sure some people wouldn't think it was a lot, but it was a huge deal to her. She scrimped and saved and tried to shop at second-hand stores to save even more. Even this tiny apartment was a conscious effort to be frugal.

Her landlord was a slimy bastard named Bob. Alabama didn't even know what his last name was. He'd only introduced himself as "Bob" before he listed the rules of his place when she'd first inquired about renting. No pets. No parties. No Subleasing. No smoking. Rent was due on the first every month. No extensions. One month deposit up front. The apartment was partially furnished, but Alabama had bought her own small bed. No way was she sleeping where someone else had done who-knew-what. She'd had to do that throughout her childhood. Alabama swore to herself once she'd graduated from high school and set out on her own that she'd never sleep on a used mattress again. So far, she'd managed it.

The one room apartment Bob advertised was really a misnomer, as the only "room" in the place was the bathroom, but that was okay with her. Alabama lived alone and didn't really need any more space.

Just as she was nodding off to sleep, there was a knock at the door. Alabama bolted upright. What the hell? No one came to her apartment. She didn't have any friends. No one ever just dropped in. Was it one of her neighbors? She'd seen the old lady who lived on the same floor as her. They'd smiled at one another, but hadn't really spoken to each other. That had to be who was at her door.

She looked down at herself. She was wearing sweats and a large T-shirt. She shrugged. It wasn't as if she needed to impress anyone. It was either her neighbor or someone who was knocking on the wrong door anyway.

Alabama went to the door and cracked it open an inch. Of course Bob hadn't spent the extra money to install doors with peepholes in them. Cheapskate.

The absolute last person she expected to see standing outside her door was Christopher. She suddenly realized she didn't even know his last name. She just stood there like an idiot staring at him through the crack in the door. What the hell was he doing here?

"Hey, Alabama. I wanted to stop by and make sure you were all right."

After staring at him for a few moments, Alabama shook herself. At the rise of his eyebrows, she bravely ignored her self-imposed no talking rule and couldn't help but ask, "How did you find me?"

She was amazed to see a rosy hue rise up his face. Holy hell, was he blushing? She'd never in a million years have thought a man like him would blush.

"Yeah, well, I figured since your name was pretty unusual you wouldn't be too hard to find…and I was right. Did you know you're the only person in Riverton named Alabama? I was all ready to ask the Wolfe's about someone who worked for them named 'Alabama' when my buddy called back about two point three seconds after I sent him your name and city. You're apparently really easy to find, probably too easy, we need to talk about that… Anyway, he found you and here I am."

Alabama could only stare at him in disbelief. Christopher actually tracked her down? Had one of his buddies track her down? Why? If he wanted to thank her he could've just called and left a message with the Wolfe's or something. Alabama had so many things she wanted to ask, but her brain wasn't cooperating.

"Yeah, so anyway, I did want to come by and thank you and see if you wanted to have a cup of coffee with me sometime."

When she didn't say anything in reply Christopher continued as if she'd agreed with him. "Okay, great. So how about I pick you up tomorrow around eleven? We'll go to that little coffee shop downtown and we'll chat." He chuckled at himself in amusement. "Well, maybe I'll chat and you'll listen." He got serious and leaned in. His voice was pitched low and demanding.

"I want to sit down with you and thank you properly for saving my life, and saving countless others as well. I don't know you, but I want to *know* you. You probably don't want any thanks, but you're getting it anyway, at least from me. Will you be here tomorrow when I come to pick you up?"

Alabama nodded immediately. When Christopher lowered his voice like that she couldn't *not* agree with anything he said. He was right, she wasn't comfortable with being the center of attention and she didn't want any thanks really. Alabama was just happy *he* was here and in one piece. She had a lot of things she had to do, the first of which was to contact the Wolfe's and figure out what she was going to do about her job, but she also wanted to sit down and have a cup of coffee with this man. Alabama just wanted to feel normal for once.

Abe straightened up and held out his hand. "We never really introduced ourselves did we? At least our full names. I'm Christopher Powers. I already told you my friends and teammates call me Abe." He waited, hoping Alabama would follow his lead.

Alabama looked down to the hand being held out to her. Christopher had well groomed nails and his hand looked strong. How could a hand look strong? She shook her head as if to clear it of her foggy thoughts. She opened the door a bit more and finally tentatively reached her hand to his. "Alabama Smith."

Abe caught her hand and shook it as she intended, but he then brought it up to his lips and gently kissed the back of it. "I'm honored to make your acquaintance." Abe couldn't believe how great her hand felt. Her *hand* for God's sake. Her nails weren't painted and he could feel the rough spots on it, obviously from the cleaning she did. But it was soft and felt so dainty enclosed in his. He never wanted to let her go. He wanted to pull her close to him and wrap his arms around her back. He resisted the urge, barely.

Alabama chuckled out loud before she could stifle it. She wasn't sure why she was laughing. She figured she was laughing at the situation—at the fact that there was a gorgeous man standing on her doorstep kissing her hand. That sort of thing just didn't happen to her.

"I'll see you in the morning, Alabama Smith. Sleep well."

Alabama watched as Christopher backed away from her door. He kept eye contact with her for as long as he could. Finally he turned around and headed down the hallway. Right before he went out of sight he looked back and winked at her. Alabama closed the door in a daze. Oh crap. Did she just agree to a date with the best looking man she'd ever met? What the hell had she done?

ABE COULDN'T SLEEP. He'd risked a lot tracking Alabama down. He usually wasn't so aggressive. Hell, who was he kidding? He couldn't remember the last time he'd had to chase a woman. It was pathetic that asking a woman out for coffee was aggressive for him. He'd gotten way too used to women throwing themselves at him. No wonder he was bored with women. He'd gotten complacent. He'd gotten lazy.

Caroline had scolded him for just that earlier that week. She'd hated Adelaide and wasn't afraid of letting him know.

Alabama was different. He couldn't put his finger on it, but somehow he knew it. It wasn't just that she was a bit shy, or that he'd had to track her down. She certainly wasn't a chatterbox, and he found he liked it. In fact he didn't think she'd said more than her name the entire time he'd been at her door. But that lack of nervous talking was calming. He didn't have to pretend to be interested in inane conversation.

Growing up as the only male in a family full of

women made solitude hard to come by. He'd never associate "calming" with women, at least he hadn't before Alabama.

He loved his sisters to death, but they sure could talk. Their family dinners were always full of stories and laughter. He'd had a great childhood. He loved his family. His sisters drove him crazy, but he wouldn't change anything about them. Susie was the youngest at twenty five. Alicia was the middle child and was twenty eight. Abe was thirty four. Abe figured the six years of age difference between him and Alicia made him the way he was today. He felt it was his responsibility to protect her. He'd spent most of his school years looking out for her and fighting her battles when he could. He'd honed his protective Alpha instincts from an early age and hadn't looked back.

He didn't begrudge his sisters or mom anything. Abe loved being the man in the family. He'd never really known his father. Even though Susie was nine years younger than him, his dad hadn't been around much. There was a reason, but it wasn't one he liked to think about.

His dad would be around for a while, then he'd be gone for a month or more. When he'd come back his mom hadn't seemed to care. Abe wasn't even really sure what he'd done for a living. A part of him felt bad about that.

All he knew was when he was eleven his mom took him aside and told him his dad had passed away. He tried not to think about what his dad had done to his mom…and him. He knew his father's actions were why he was the way he was today and Abe figured some psychologist would have a field day analyzing him and his protective personality. They'd link it back to his dad, and try to get him to talk about it, but he was who he was and he wasn't going to change.

Abe had always looked after his family. Family was the most important thing in his life and he'd protect them to the end of his days. Nothing was more important than his sisters and mom. Abe once brought a woman home for a family dinner and at the end of the night knew the relationship was over. His date had been rude and hadn't veiled her contempt at his mom's homeliness. He knew he turned sappy when he was around his sisters and mom, but he loved them more than anything and he'd be damned if anyone would feel it was all right to belittle that. He'd dumped her on the way home and wouldn't listen to her attempts at explaining her words had come out wrong.

He hoped like hell Alabama would get along with his family. It was way too early to be thinking anywhere along those lines, but Abe couldn't help it. He knew he'd bring her around to meet them before too long. He hated it was a test of sorts, but he was getting old enough now to want what he wanted and the hell with anyone who thought he was inflexible.

Abe was ready to have someone of his own, especially after seeing Caroline and Matthew and how happy they were. He hadn't even thought about Adelaide being his. He'd known he was biding his time with her. Adelaide was good in bed and had been enough for him. Other than her being catty and pretentious, he hadn't even known what it was that really bothered him about her or any other relationship he'd been in.

It struck Abe in the middle of that inferno with flames licking at the walls and the air in the room running out—what it was that made Alabama different from any other woman he'd ever dated. Abe's entire life he'd taken care of others. He didn't begrudge anyone that, it was the way he was. It was second nature for him to open doors, buckle a woman's seatbelt, pull out chairs, and basically be courteous and helpful. Abe's job with the SEALs only reinforced that protectiveness. He was always the one rushing in to save someone else. He performed best on missions where they'd been sent in to save someone's life or rescue them. It was his job, his duty, and he did it well.

But Alabama's simple act of taking the time to douse him with water and find a coat to cover him up with floored him. Alabama startled the hell out of him when she'd dumped the pitcher of water on his head, but luckily he'd known immediately what she was doing. He'd never have forgiven himself if he'd retaliated against her for thinking she was a threat.

But what sealed the deal for Abe was when they were crawling across the floor and Alabama had reached back and handed him something to breathe through. She hadn't said anything; she hadn't wanted anything from him. She'd simply acted to do something *for* him. That was it.

Abe doubted she even realized how momentous her actions were to him. No one "took care" of him. He took care of others, always. Even his mom hadn't taken care of him in a long time, since he was little. He still called her every week when he wasn't on a mission to make sure she was all right, to see if she needed anything. He'd do little chores around the house and generally make sure all was right in her world.

It was the same with his sisters. Abe would always take care of them. He loved them, of course, but it was more than that. He didn't want them to suffer any hardship if he could prevent it. He went all out on their birthdays and the holidays.

But no one took care of him. Abe hadn't even noticed it until Alabama and that damn napkin she'd handed him. Even when he was sick, he cared for himself. Once when he'd gotten in a minor car wreck, his family and SEAL team were there in the hospital for him, but as soon as he was discharged, they'd gone back to their homes and lives. Abe didn't feel slighted at the time, but now? That damn napkin meant everything to him. He wished he still had it. He'd frame it and put it on his wall.

He wanted to ask her why she'd done it. The thing that really struck him was that they were in the middle of a life-and-death situation and she'd done it. Hell, they didn't even *know* each other. Abe couldn't name one other woman that would've taken the time look out for him in that same situation. It was human nature to look out for yourself first. He'd seen it over and over on some of the rescue missions he'd been on and in all the foreign countries he'd been to over the years.

He chuckled bitterly. Adelaide certainly hadn't cared how he was or what he was doing. It wasn't until they were outside and safe and the EMT had come over to them, that she'd even tried to pretend to have any kind of concern for him. It had been too late for that. Way too late.

Abe still had a lot of unanswered questions, but the bottom line was that he had an urgent drive to find Alabama. He had to get to know her better. He had to see if this feeling was mutual. Tex had made fun of him and wanted to know more about the mysterious Alabama, but Abe told him to mind his own business.

Abe had hunted her down and was taking her out

for coffee in the morning. It was almost pathetic how excited he was. He hoped to get to know her better. Abe wanted to know everything. How old she was, where she was from, if she had brothers or sisters…hell, he wanted to know anything she'd tell him. He chuckled to himself. He'd be lucky if she said anything. Alabama was quiet as a mouse. He couldn't deny a part of him wanted to be the one to bring her out of her shell. To hear her call out his name in her quiet melodious voice while be brought her to orgasm.

Hell, Abe was already picturing them in bed together and they hadn't even had a first date. He tried to reign in his overactive imagination. There'd be time for that later. For now he had to think about how he was going to get Alabama to go on a second date with him.

Chapter Five

ALABAMA DIDN'T SLEEP well that night. She tossed and turned and couldn't stop wondering why Christopher had asked her out for coffee. She worried he might be doing it on a dare, or because he thought she was a challenge. She really had no idea why he'd ask *her* out. Adelaide was beautiful, and it was obvious they were dating. Was he cheating on Adelaide? If so, Alabama would be extremely disillusioned. She wanted him to be the gallant man she'd dreamed about.

She started worrying again why he'd be asking her out. Once in high school one of the boys on the football team had asked her if she wanted to meet him at the skating rink. She'd been ecstatic. She wasn't the type of person guys noticed. She'd spent a long time getting ready and trying to make herself look as pretty as possible. She'd even shown up at the rink early, she'd been so excited.

As she sat and waited for the boy to show up, she'd quickly realized it was a set up. Every other football player had been there along with most of the cheerleading squad. They'd skate by her table and giggle and laugh. After an hour of sitting by herself enduring the stares and giggles, she'd slunk out of the building, humiliated. She'd found out later it had been a type of initiation for the guy. The rest of the team had dared him to ask out the school "weirdo." He had, and the joke lived on in infamy in the halls of her high school.

Alabama had honestly thought he'd asked her out because he saw something in her worth dating. It wasn't until she was out of high school that she'd dared to try to go out with a guy again. Unfortunately, that had been a disaster as well. She'd lost her virginity to that man, only to find out he'd been trying to make his exgirlfriend jealous, and he'd really not even liked her all that much. Of course he'd "stooped" to sleeping with her, even though he hadn't wanted to see her again. The whole experience was embarrassing and just another disappointment in a long line of them when it came to men.

With Alabama's history she just couldn't understand why Christopher would ask her out and be serious about it. She was just a cleaning lady, he was….hell, she had no idea what he was, but she was sure whatever it was, he was good at it.

After a few hours of twisting and turning in her bed and worrying herself sick, she made the decision that he probably asked her to coffee to some way to get back at Adelaide. She decided she just wouldn't answer the door when he got there in the morning. She'd pretend to not be at home. He'd knock then go away. Alabama could avoid any embarrassment and humiliation he was sure to be trying to pile on.

Alabama was way too nervous to eat any breakfast in the morning. She'd gotten up very early and paced the house. She finally decided to put on a pair of jeans and a long sleeved V-neck shirt. She wasn't expecting to see Christopher, but just in case, she wanted to be prepared.

At the last minute Alabama figured she probably should've left the house altogether instead of staying inside and pretending to be out, but it was too late by the time she'd thought about it.

At ten fifty five sharp, Christopher knocked on her door. Alabama sat on her couch staring at the door, wishing he'd give up and leave. He knocked again and she heard his voice through the door.

"Alabama? Are you there? Come on, sweetheart. Open the door."

Alabama stayed silent and bit her lip in trepidation.

"I know you're in there. Open the door and talk to me, well, at least let me see you so I know you're all right. If you don't come to the door I'll assume you're sicker from the fire than you let on and I'll have to break the door to get in to make sure you're okay."

Alabama wrestled with herself. Damn. She had to open it. She didn't want to have to pay to have the stupid door replaced. She figured he'd do just what he said; he'd break it down if she didn't open it. Christopher was certainly strong enough to do it without even breaking a sweat.

She walked quickly to the door and cracked it open, just as she had the night before. Christopher was leaning against the doorjamb looking way sexier than anyone had the right to look. He was wearing a faded pair of jeans and a scruffy pair of tennis shoes. He had on a polo shirt with a few buttons undone at the collar and a light windbreaker was over his shoulder to top off his outfit. His hair was messy, as if he'd run his hand through it a couple of times.

"Hey, Alabama. You ready to go?" Abe acted as if he hadn't just told her he'd break her door down if she didn't answer it.

Alabama knew she should be scared of him, he'd just kinda threatened her after all, but she couldn't be. She knew he wouldn't hurt her. How she knew that she had no idea, but she did. She nodded at him and backed away from the door to get her purse.

Abe gently pushed the door open and took a step inside her apartment. It wasn't very big, but it was clean and homey looking. She had placemats set out on the tiny kitchen table and there were two stools pushed under the table. There was a vase with some wildflowers in it. The one room didn't have a lot of furniture in it, but it still seemed a bit cramped. There was a small bed up against one wall with a blanket thrown over it. There was a tattered loveseat couch across from the bed. It was obviously a second hand piece of furniture because it had a sheet thrown over it and he could see the legs on the thing were chopped off.

There was a small television across from the couch that was sitting on an, again, obviously second hand table. Even though he could tell many of the things she had were hand-me-downs, it didn't look ragged. Alabama had gone to great lengths to try to clean and polish everything up. She'd put in a lot of effort into her home and he actually liked it much more than Adelaide's large, polished, perfect apartment.

Abe watched as Alabama walked over to the kitchen counter and grabbed a small purse. When she turned around he couldn't help but be dazzled by her. The V-neck T-shirt she was wearing wasn't provocative at all, but she still looked sexy as hell in it. He could see a hint of cleavage and being a breast man, he could tell she was all natural. He hadn't realized until this very moment how much he disliked fake boobs.

Alabama turned back toward Christopher, who was now standing just inside her front door. She was embarrassed he'd seen her little apartment. She knew it was nothing special, but it was all she could afford. She'd worked hard at finding just the right furniture for her home. She'd spent a few weeks going to the different thrift shops and garage sales to find what suited her. It wasn't new, but it was comfortable, that was all that mattered to her.

But now, looking at it through Christopher's eyes Alabama was embarrassed. It was old. It was beat up, and it was obvious. She headed back toward him looking at the floor hoping she'd make it through the morning and whatever humiliation was in store.

Abe took Alabama by the elbow when she got close to him. "I like your place, Alabama." He was surprised when she snorted in response. He smiled. God that was cute. "No seriously, you've done a great job at making this place comfortable. Oh I know, it isn't fancy, but it's you. It's cozy and lived in. I'd much prefer that to living in a place that was hard and stilted and way too fancy. You've done a good job."

Alabama looked up at him. Was he serious? She saw the small grin on his face as he looked down at her. Whoa. He *was* serious. "Thanks," she said softly returning his smile with a tentative one of her own.

Satisfied that she'd taken his compliment gracefully, Abe steered her out the door and held out his hand. "Keys." He chuckled at Alabama's look of confusion. "Give me your keys, sweetheart. I'll lock your door for you."

Alabama looked down at the keys she was holding tightly in her hands. Why did he want to lock her door? She could do it. She didn't say anything though, and dropped her key ring into his outstretched hand and watched as he put the key in the lock and turned it. When he put her keys into his pocket after he was done, she couldn't keep quiet.

"Give them back," she said as sternly as she could, not looking into his eyes and trying not to panic.

Abe had put her keys in his pocket without even thinking about it. He'd naturally kept them, planning on being around to open her door for her when he brought her home again. At her tone of voice he took a second look. Alabama was panicking. It was obvious, especially to him, as he'd been trained to read body language. He immediately put his hand in his pocket to retrieve her keychain.

"Don't panic, sweet, here they are. I'm sorry; I didn't mean to scare you. I didn't even think about it. I wasn't trying to keep you from your home."

Alabama breathed in a sigh of relief and closed her fingers around her keys again. He was right, she *had* been panicking. She'd once stayed at a foster home where the parents didn't give the foster kids keys to the house. She'd had to sit on the stoop all the time waiting for them to get home and unlock the door. She felt like a stranger in her own home. One evening she'd been locked out all night because they'd gone on an overnight trip and hadn't told her they were leaving. She didn't like to ever be without a way to get into her house ever since. She nodded at him in embarrassment and thanks, and dropped her keys into her purse.

Abe walked them to his car, an ordinary four door sedan. For some reason Alabama thought he might have owned something a bit more flashy.

He must have read her confusion because he told her without a bit of embarrassment, "I know it's not anything fancy, but I prefer reliable over flash."

When they got to the passenger side of the car Abe opened it and waited until she sat down. Then he grabbed the seatbelt and handed it to her.

Alabama took the belt without a word and watched as Christopher walked around the front of the car. She continued watching him as he sat in the driver's seat and got comfortable.

When he looked over at her and saw she was looking at him he smiled a small smile and asked, "What?"

Alabama just smiled shyly at him and shook her head. She couldn't put into words what she was feeling, even if she wasn't reticent to talk.

Abe didn't push the issue; he just started the car and pulled away from the apartment complex. They didn't talk during the ride, but the silence wasn't uncomfortable. Alabama felt safe with him. He was a good driver. He wasn't reckless, he wasn't driving the speed limit, but he also wasn't being a speed demon.

They pulled up to the local coffee shop. It was a cute little building and the shop was called simply *Coffee and More*. Alabama had stopped in a few times in the past and enjoyed the little snacks and the flavored coffees they offered.

Abe parked the car and turned to Alabama. "Stay put, I'll come around and open your door for you." He waited until Alabama nodded before getting out and walking around to her side. He opened her door and held her elbow as she climbed out of the passenger seat.

On their way to the front door, Alabama felt Christopher's hand on the small of her back. He wasn't groping her, just confidently leading her where he wanted her to go, without being in front of her. It felt good. It'd been so long since she'd been touched. She led a solitary existence and hadn't ever been touched affectionately. She hadn't missed it until right this moment with Christopher's hand warming her back.

Abe opened the door and followed Alabama into the small shop. The décor was just as cute as the outside of the shop.

One side of the room had the counter and the kitchen area. The rest of the room was filled with seats. There were a few loveseats with big fluffy pillows. There were also some tables scattered around the room. Some were square and others were circular shaped. There was even a long table against the wall that had electrical outlets along the back side, for those that wanted to sit and use their computer while they enjoyed their coffee. The floor had two big circular rugs in bright colors. It brightened up the room and made it seem more homey.

The pictures on the wall were obviously done by children. They were framed and matted as if they were done by a master painter. Alabama had heard the owner held a contest every year and whichever child won got to see their picture up on her wall. The place was comfortable. The music wasn't playing loudly. It was a place people could relax in. She'd always loved the coffee shop and was happy Christopher picked it.

She still wasn't sure why he'd chosen to bring her here, but for now she was going with it.

"What can I get for you, sweet?" he asked leading her up to the counter.

"Vanilla latte, please."

"No problem. Do you want anything to snack on?" At the shake of her head he told her, "Okay, I'll take care of this. Go ahead and choose a place you want to sit, I'll be there in a sec."

Alabama hesitated for just a moment. She felt as if she should offer to pay or something, but she knew he'd probably be offended. She mentally shrugged. It was only a coffee after all.

She headed over to a small circular table that was near the wall on the other side of the restaurant and sat facing the room. Alabama watched as Christopher strode over to the table not too much later. He had two coffees and a small bag.

When he got to the table, Alabama expected him to take a seat and get right down to business telling her what he wanted her to know.

Abe put the drinks on the table and set the bag of muffins down as well. When he didn't sit down Alabama looked up at him. Abe looked uncomfortable. He ran his hand over the back of his neck. Finally he said, "Sweet, I don't want you to feel uncomfortable here, but I can't sit with my back to the room."

Alabama didn't understand. She gave him a quizzical look.

"I'm a Navy SEAL. I've been trained to be aware of my surroundings at all times. I can't sit with my back to the room. I need to sit where I can see what's going on. Will you switch seats with me?"

Alabama got it. Of *course,* he was in the military. She should've known. She'd taken the seat with her back to the wall, leaving the chair on the other side of the small table for him. She quickly stood up and mumbled, "Sorry," as she went to scoot around Christopher to take the other chair.

Abe blocked her maneuver and put his hand under her chin, forcing her to look up at him. "Don't apologize, sweet, you didn't know. We could both sit on that side if you wanted." He didn't give her a chance to agree or disagree, but put his hand at her waist and gently nudged her back from the table. He grabbed the chair she'd just vacated and pushed it over a foot. Then he leaned over and took hold of the other chair and pulled it to sit against the wall next to the first one.

Then he again put his hand at her waist and steered her into the furthest chair. After she'd sat down, he settled himself in the chair next to her. It was a close fit. His knee brushed against hers and his arm touched hers as they sat. He reached over to the bag and brought out two muffins. He put one on a napkin in front of her and placed the bigger of the pastries on it. He pushed the vanilla latte over in front of her before getting his own food set.

Then he turned to her and said, "So, tell me everything about yourself. I want to know it all."

Chapter Six

A LABAMA LOOKED AT Christopher in shock. Tell him everything about her? No way in hell. He didn't really want to know.

At her look of disbelief, Abe chuckled. "Too fast? Okay, how about if I go first?"

Alabama didn't know what was going on. She thought he just wanted to thank her. Now he wanted to know everything about her? And he wanted to tell her about him? She couldn't wrap her mind around it all.

"You know my name is Christopher Powers. I have two sisters, both younger than me. I'm thirty four years old. I'm a Navy SEAL. My buddies call me Abe. I love my job because I love my country. I don't like what I see while I'm doing my job sometimes though. I've never been married, never even come close. I've had one serious girlfriend in my life, when I was sixteen." He paused and smiled then continued. "I've seen a lot in my life, and I've done a lot of macho things, but nothing impressed me more than you in the middle of that room burning down around us. You kept your head, saved a lot of lives, saved *my* life. Thank you."

Alabama didn't know what to say. She looked away from him down at the table and the muffin she'd been shredding with her fingers while he talked.

Abe reached out and put his finger beneath her chin and raised her head so she'd look him in the eyes once more. God, she was amazing. Most of the women he'd known in the past would have simpered and cooed and taken his words as an invitation to snuggle up to him and get closer to him. Not Alabama. His words made her uncomfortable and she tried to hide from him. The skin under his finger was warm and smooth. He wanted to cup her cheek in his hand, but knew that would be too much for her right now. Soon.

"I didn't say that to embarrass you, sweet. I just wanted to let you know how much I appreciate what you did for me. I'm a big bad SEAL, no one takes care of me. But when you did it, it felt great. So thank you."

Alabama just nodded. God. This was…she didn't know what this was. Every time he called her "sweet", she felt her heart lurch. She'd never had a man speak to her as if she was important, as if he didn't want to be anywhere other than in her company. Goose bumps broke out over her arms. Christopher's hand felt good on her skin. She wanted to lean into him, to feel his hand running over her hair, but she didn't know him.

She figured he was just grateful to her, he'd just said so after all.

"I...you're welcome." She managed to squeak out.

Abe let go of her chin and reached for her hand. He threaded his fingers with hers and squeezed her hand. "Okay, your turn. Tell me about yourself."

Alabama froze. She couldn't. She wasn't interesting at all. She looked around nervously out of habit. She'd always made sure growing up Mama wasn't anywhere nearby when she needed to say something. Alabama hated that she still did it today, but she couldn't break the habit. There were just too many times she'd been caught unaware by Mama to be able to stop herself. Seeing no one that resembled Mama, Alabama cautiously turned back to Christopher.

"I'm Alabama Smith. I'm thirty. I've lived here for several years. I don't have any siblings or family. It's just me." She stopped. What else could she tell him? She didn't have anything else. She didn't have a good job. She was just...her.

"Go on, sweet," Abe encouraged. "Tell me more. I want to know everything."

"That's it. There isn't much to know about me."

"I highly doubt that. Alabama, you're amazing. You've made a home out of a tiny little apartment that most people would scoff at. You saved the lives of dozens of people this week. You're beautiful. I want to know everything about you. Your favorite color, your favorite food, what you like to read, where you went to school…everything. Maybe not today, but I'd like to see you again. I want to get to know you."

Alabama could only gape at him. What the hell did this gorgeous man want with her? Was he messing with her head? Like high school? She couldn't stop the next words from coming out of her mouth.

"Did you lose a bet?"

Abe watched as Alabama blushed. She was so damn cute, but he didn't like the implications of her question. He squeezed her hand again and ran his thumb over the back of her hand. He definitely didn't like her lack of self-esteem and what might have happened in her life to make her that way.

"No sweet. I'm here because I see you. I'm here because I like what I see. I want to get to know you better because no one has ever affected me the way you have. I'm not a boy who plays games, I'm a man. I'm a man who saw a woman who caught his interest, and wants to get to know her better."

"I don't get it." Alabama was frustrated she couldn't put into words what she meant. She knew what she looked like. She wasn't a troll, but she also didn't look like Adelaide. She wasn't fashionable, she wasn't gorgeous, she wasn't…she just wasn't like the women she imagined he'd be with.

Shifting so he sat sideways in his chair, Abe turned Alabama as well. He just reached out and shifted her chair with her sitting in it. He scooted his chair closer to her so she had no choice but to part her legs to give him room. Their position was intimate. He took hold of her other hand and they sat facing each other. Alabama could feel her breathing speed up and her heart race. Holy moly. He was intense, but intense in a good way.

"Alabama, look at me. Does it look like I have a problem finding a woman?" He wasn't being cocky; he just wanted to make a point to her. When she shook her head emphatically, he chuckled and then continued.

"Exactly. I'm here because I want to be here. Women like Adelaide are nice to look at sure, but they aren't nice inside. They want me because I'm a SEAL. They want me because I have muscles. They want me because they think I can give them something. I don't think that's the way you see me. Am I right?"

Alabama slowly nodded her head. That definitely wasn't the way she saw him. If she had any brains she'd choose a man who was nerdy and would fade into the woodwork, just like her. She had no idea why she had the instant attraction to Christopher, she only knew she did.

"Adelaide isn't a good person, Alabama. I knew it before last night and was going to break it off with her. She only invited me to that shindig because she wanted to show me off. But you, you *saw* me. Even when I was being an ass, you forgave me on the spot." Abe switched topics abruptly, trying to get his point across to the shy woman sitting across from him.

"I've saved hundreds of lives. I've gone into situations you'd only think about in your nightmares. The fire that night was nothing compared to what I've lived through. I saw the direction the other people you spoke with were crawling and was about to head that way myself when you appeared out of the smoke. No one, other than my mother when I was a baby, and my teammates, have ever had my back the way you did. You put your life at risk for me. *Me*. You think I didn't notice that you came across the room to me instead of getting your ass out of there? I did. That's why I want to get to know you. That's why I think you're so much better than women like Adelaide. You're a good person inside and that's what I saw that night. That's who I want to get to know. You'll let me right? You'll let me take you out on a real date?"

Alabama could only stare at the beautiful man in front of her. She still didn't one hundred percent believe he was telling the truth. She was just Alabama. A broken woman who'd had a crappy childhood, but she couldn't help but *want* to believe him. *Want* to have the fairytale.

There was no denying Christopher was a beautiful man. He was tall. She'd prefer his hair be a bit longer, but couldn't deny the short military cut looked good on him. He was muscular all over. He probably didn't have an ounce of fat on him anywhere. Christopher was definitely fit and ready to go on whatever mission he and his team were called on. But besides all the outside trappings, she wanted to believe he was a good man. When he'd spoken about his sisters she could hear the pride in his voice. Alabama knew being on a SEAL team was one of the toughest jobs in the military. He put himself on the line every day for his country, and most of the time no one would ever know how dangerous his job was.

"Thank you for your service to our country," she blurted out before thinking. Alabama mentally slapped her forehead. God, she was such a dork. There he was asking if he could see her again and she'd gone and said that.

Abe simply smiled and brought one of their clasped hands up to his mouth. He kissed the back of her hand and left his lips there for a moment while looking into her eyes. "Thank you sweet. Now…about that date…"

"Yes."

The smile that broke out over his face was dazzling. "That wasn't so hard now was it? We can exchange cell numbers and I'll make the arrangements and call you." At her immediate frown he asked, "What? What's wrong?"

"I don't have a cell," she admitted sheepishly. She couldn't afford one. The hundred dollars a month that it cost was too much. Alabama was embarrassed. *Everyone* had a cell phone these days. Since she didn't have a lot of friends she didn't see the need. She had a land-line in her apartment, but hadn't ever owned a cell phone.

"But you have a phone? At home?" At her nod, Abe continued. "No problem then, just give me that number and I'll give you mine and I'll call you. Okay?"

Christopher could tell she was embarrassed about not having a mobile phone and he tried to downplay it as best he could. He was surprised actually. He'd never met anyone that didn't have a cell phone. There was no way he'd let her know though. He didn't want to embarrass her any more than she already was.

Abe didn't like the thought of her not having a way to contact someone in case she had an emergency. Anything could happen, her car could break down, she could have an accident, someone could break in…the bad things flashed through his mind one after another. He thought about Caroline, hell, someone *had* broken into her apartment. If she hadn't had her cell phone the police might not have gotten there in time.

Abe couldn't help but see Alabama stranded some-where with no way of getting a hold of anyone…specifically him, when she needed help.

Seeing the look on his face made Alabama want to explain. "I have plans to get one of those pay-as-you-go phones for emergencies, I just haven't yet."

"It's okay sweet. No need to explain to me. People today are way too dependent on cell phones. They don't stop to actually talk to people, always looking down at their little screen to see what the next tweet is from some overpriced actor in Hollywood."

He smiled at Alabama when he saw her relax a bit. God, he wanted nothing more than to wrap her up in his arms and take her home and hide away from the world. Nothing in his life had prepared him for her. But he wasn't backing off, no matter how much he was pushing his luck. And she'd be getting that phone before she knew it, that was for sure. He'd take care of it for her.

"Okay, so I'll call you tonight?" Waiting for her affirmative nod, he then continued. "I'll plan something for Friday. Are you busy that day? I have to check in on base in the morning for PT, but then I have the weekend free, as long as we don't get called in. That's always a possibility. Does that bother you?"

Alabama thought about it. Did it bother her? Yes, but not in the way he was probably thinking. She looked around furtively again, checking to make sure it was safe to speak, then told him with more honesty then she probably should've shared at that point in their relationship, whatever that relationship was.

"Yes, but not because you won't be able to take me out, but because if you get sent on a mission I know it'll be dangerous. And I'll worry about you."

Not liking the way she constantly scanned the room before speaking, Abe put that aside for the moment, instead concentrating on what she'd said. "Thanks for worrying about me sweet. I'm trained. My teammates are trained. They have my back and I have theirs. I know we don't know each other that well yet, but understand this. I'll do everything in my power to get back safely. I think I've just discovered another reason to make sure I come home safe."

Alabama blushed hotly. Holy crapola. He was intense. This whole conversation was intense. It was crazy. How in the hell could he feel those things about her when he didn't even know her? Hell, how could she feel that way about him?

Abe loved the blush that crept up Alabama's face. Jesus, she was cute. Trying to lighten the mood he reluctantly let go of her hands and scooted his chair back a bit. "Come on, let's finish up our breakfast and I'll take you home. Unfortunately, I have some things I have to do on base today, but I'll call you later tonight."

Alabama leaned on the inside of her apartment door and listened as Christopher walked away down the shabby hallway of her apartment complex. They'd finished their muffins and coffees and he'd brought her home. He'd insisted on escorting her back up to her doorway. She was nervous, wondering if he'd kiss her. He hadn't, but he had taken her face in his hands and leaned his forehead against hers briefly.

"Lock the door behind you sweet. Okay? I want to hear the chain going on."

It was an odd thing to say in such an intimate position, but all she could do was nod. Christopher had taken a deep breath and stood up straight, not taking his hands off her face. Finally he'd run one hand up and over her hair and the other moved to lightly squeeze her shoulder. "I'll talk to you later."

Alabama knew he'd waited outside her door until he'd heard her locking the door and putting the security chain on. Then he'd walked away down the hall.

She slid down the door holding her knees. Whoa. This morning had been surreal. She smiled to herself. Good surreal. No, *great* surreal.

Chapter Seven

ALABAMA HAD MADE it through the day on auto pilot. She hadn't contacted the Wolfe's yet about her job, but it was first thing on her to-do list for the next day. She'd been putting it off, but couldn't any longer.

She piddled around all day doing nothing important in her apartment. She cleaned it from top to bottom, did all of her laundry, including her bed sheets and towels, she'd even scrubbed the toilet. She'd tried to read for a while, but the romances she usually read just weren't holding her attention.

Would Christopher call? He *said* he'd call, but she still didn't really believe he would. Even with everything he'd told her that morning, it was hard for her to believe. At one point she put in the movie *Drop Dead Gorgeous* to try to keep her anticipation down. She'd bought a bunch of movies at a garage sale once, and had never regretted it. She'd gotten some great oldies including *The Princess Bride*, *Ever After,* and even some of the *Little House on the Prairie* seasons.

Alabama thought about the supposed-impending call. While it was true she had an issue talking with people, speaking on the phone was easier…as long as she could close herself off in a small room. She felt safe that way. If she was in her own house, locked away where Mama couldn't possibly find her, she was okay with talking. Alabama knew she probably needed therapy of some kind, but it just wasn't a priority at this time for her.

Just as the movie got to the point where the first pageant was starting, her phone rang. It scared the crap out of her, even though she was half expecting it. It had to be Christopher, no one else called her. Ever.

Alabama stopped the movie, grabbed her cordless phone and climbed into her small bed. She looked around the apartment one last time making sure she was alone. Of course she was. She was always alone.

She snuggled down under the covers and lay on her side and huddled into herself before finally pushing the talk button on the phone.

"Hello?"

"Hey, sweet. It's Abe."

Alabama giggled. "I know. I recognized your voice."

"You should do that more often," Abe told her.

"What?"

"Laugh. You have a beautiful laugh."

Alabama blushed; even when he wasn't in front of her he could embarrass her. "Thanks, I think. How was your day?"

Abe was thrilled she was talking to him. He wasn't sure she would after getting to know her a bit that morning. She wasn't a talker, that was obvious. He was half afraid he'd be talking to himself when he called. He was pleasantly surprised. "It was good. I worked out with my team, sat in on a few meetings, then had dinner with my friend Wolf and his woman, Ice."

"Wolf? Ice?" Alabama asked.

"Yeah, remember how I told you I was called Abe? Well, Matthew's nickname is Wolf. His girlfriend's name is Caroline, but she earned the moniker 'Ice.' Everyone on the team has a nickname. Most of the time it has to do with something about that person. Matthew earned the name Wolf because of the way he ate while training to become a SEAL. He'd scarf down all his food and come back for more. He was always wolfing down his food. The name stuck."

Alabama loved hearing Christopher talk about his friends. He had such passion in his voice. It was obvious he loved what he did and really liked the people he worked with. "Why Ice? Is she on your team too?"

"Not exactly. We met her a little bit ago when we were flying to Virginia. She saved all the lives on the plane we were on. Terrorists had drugged the ice they used to make the drinks with and were planning on hijacking the plane. She's a chemist and realized what was going on. Wolf happened to be sitting next to her and was able to let us know what was going down and we were able to foil the plan. They went through some other shit too, but all's well that ends well. They're blissfully happy and I'm proud to call both of them my friends."

Alabama smiled. She was scared to death to hear that he'd almost died, but happy he had such great friends. "I remember seeing that on the news. I'm so glad you guys are all okay. Why are you called Abe?"

Abe laughed. "The guys started calling me that because I can't stand it when people lie. I'd much rather people be honest with me. Even if it's crap I don't want to hear, I want the truth."

Alabama hesitated. She wasn't sure she wanted to be one hundred percent honest with him. She was ashamed with her history. On one hand she knew it wasn't her fault, but if her own mama didn't want her, how and why would anyone else?

"Sweet? You still there?"

"I'm here."

"You okay?"

"Yeah."

"You're freaked aren't you?" When she didn't say anything Abe went on. "Please don't be. I don't expect you to spill your guts with me right off. I do want to know everything about you, but I don't want you to lie to me. When you feel comfortable enough, you can talk to me."

"How do you know I have something to spill in the first place?"

"Sweet, I've been around enough people with Post-traumatic Stress Disorder to recognize it when I see it." When she started to interrupt him to protest, he wouldn't let her. "No, it's okay. I don't know what happened to you, but it doesn't matter to me. I like you. I like that you're soft-spoken and think about your words before you say them. I don't like that you look around the room to see who's there before you speak, and I hope you'll tell me about that someday, but rest assured, I won't hold it against you. Okay?"

"Are you for real?" Alabama couldn't believe what she was hearing. How could this man know her, with-out really knowing her? It was eerie really.

"I'm for real, sweet." Christopher knew Alabama was getting freaked out, and it was the last thing he wanted to do. "Tell me about your day," he changed the subject, hoping to make her feel more comfortable.

Alabama talked to Christopher for two hours straight. They talked about nothing really, non-important stuff that most people spoke about when they were getting to know each other. She learned his favorite food was a thick juicy steak, and he learned that she loved to go the movies by herself on the weekends and get lost in a good thriller.

"I've really loved talking to you," Abe told her quietly. "But I do need to get going. I've got training in the morning and you need to get some sleep."

"Okay, Christopher. Thank you for calling. I've really enjoyed it."

"It was my pleasure. The only way this would've been better is if we'd been face to face. I'll get back with you soon about our date on Friday, all right?"

"All right."

"Sleep well, sweet. I'll be thinking about you."

"Good night."

"Bye."

Alabama clicked off the phone and held it to her chest. She'd never felt like this in all her life. She felt as if she mattered. She'd never mattered to anyone before. It felt good.

Chapter Eight

ALABAMA HAD JUST spoken with Stacey Wolfe. She'd been glad to hear from her and had expressed her thanks for what she'd done to help save lives the night of the fire. She'd reassured Alabama that she still had a job. The Wolfe's were working on renting a building near the one that had burned down until they could rebuild. Within a week they'd be ready and Alabama could go back to work.

The company was even going to pay her for the week of work she wouldn't be doing. It was more than generous of them. Alabama almost didn't know what to do with the surprising time off. She would've preferred to have stayed busy so she wouldn't have to think about her upcoming date.

She hadn't seen Christopher since their coffee date, but they'd talked on the phone two more times. The first time it was a short conversation. Christopher had called in between meetings just to say hello. Alabama had been so bamboozled, she hadn't had much to say, but luckily Christopher didn't seem to mind.

The second time was another late night phone call and they talked for another couple of hours. Alabama learned more about his sisters and mom and how much they meant to him. He'd even told her he wanted them to meet her. He knew he'd made her uncomfortable and had rushed to reassure her that they'd love her.

They'd talked for a bit more before ending the call. Alabama even admitted to him partly why she was able to talk to him on the phone, but wasn't comfortable talking in public. She'd told him she didn't have to worry about if anyone was around listening to her or judging her. Christopher had tried to tell her that it didn't matter what others thought about her, but since that wasn't the only reason she was more comfortable talking to him on the phone in the safety of her own house, Alabama didn't argue with him.

Christopher had again told her that he'd be thinking about her before he let her hang up the phone.

Now it was Friday and time for their date. Christopher wouldn't tell her much about where they were going, he'd only told her to be sure to wear comfortable clothes and to bring a sweatshirt of some sort.

Abe was feeling antsy. He hadn't felt this way about a woman in a long time. His buddies, especially Wolf, had teased him unmercifully. They'd all wanted to meet Alabama, but he'd told them they'd have to wait. He knew Alabama was shy around others and didn't want her to be overwhelmed with his friends before he could make sure she was his.

Abe planned an interesting day for them, knowing if she'd enjoyed the day, she really was the woman for him. He felt a little bad about testing Alabama the way he was planning, but he'd been snowed too many times by women who he'd thought liked him for him, but were only pretending interest in what he liked. Deep down he knew Alabama wasn't like that, so this wasn't so much a test as it was a way to spend some quality time with an amazing woman.

Abe shook his head as he pulled up to her apartment complex. It really was a piece of crap. He wouldn't say anything her though, because he figured she didn't make a lot of money. He hoped she'd open up to him today and tell him more about herself. He didn't even know what she did for a living, except that it had something to do with Wolfe Realty.

He moved the package on the seat next to him to the backseat before exiting his car and walking up to her floor. He knocked once and the door was opened almost immediately. He smiled. She looked great. Alabama was wearing a pair of well-worn jeans and a fitted V-neck T-shirt, the kind she usually wore. It was a deep purple color and plunged deep into her chest. Holding a white sweatshirt over one arm, she'd dressed just like he'd asked. He loved it.

Alabama was nervous as all get out. She had no idea what they'd be doing today, but she trusted Christopher. She probably shouldn't, but hell, if she couldn't trust a Navy SEAL, who could she trust? Alabama tried on three different shirts before settling on the purple one. She thought it made her chest look "perkier," and she'd always loved the color.

Christopher looked good. He was wearing a pair of khaki cargo pants and a long sleeved shirt. It wasn't tight like he was trying to show off, but it was snug. Alabama could see the definition of his arms. He was built. God, was he built. He was wearing a pair of combat boots on his feet. He was leaning against the doorframe of her apartment when she opened the door. If he'd been selling something, she would've bought whatever it was on the spot.

Alabama stepped out of her apartment and wasn't surprised when Christopher held out his hand for her keys. She remembered he'd done that the first time he'd picked her up too. She dropped her keys in his hand and watched as he locked her door. When he was finished, instead of putting the keychain in his pocket as he'd done the last time, Christopher turned and held it out to her. She smiled shyly at him as she took the keys and put them in her purse. He'd remembered how she wasn't comfortable in letting him keep her keys and hadn't pushed the issue. She liked that about him. Heck, so far she'd liked everything about Christopher.

Abe took Alabama's elbow as they walked down the hall. He winked at the old lady who was peeking out her door at them as they walked by. She winked back and smiled, then closed her door after they'd passed.

As they settled into the car, Abe looked at Alabama. She hadn't asked where they were going, although he could tell she was curious.

Before starting the car, he leaned behind them and picked up the package. He handed it to Alabama and leaned one arm on the steering wheel and watched her.

Alabama looked at Christopher in bewilderment. He'd gotten her a present?

"Go ahead, open it." Abe urged gently.

Alabama carefully peeled back the paper on the package and looked into the box. It'd been a long time since she'd gotten a gift. Hell, she couldn't remember when anyone had ever wrapped something up for her. She almost wanted to keep it wrapped and stare at it all day, but Alabama knew she'd look like a freak if she did that.

After lingering over opening the gift for as long as she could she stared down at what he'd given her. It was a phone. Not one of the crazy expensive smart phones, he must've known she wouldn't accept one of those, but a flip phone that you paid for as you used the minutes.

Alabama bit her lip and tried not to cry. Mama hadn't ever celebrated Christmas with her and certainly hadn't bought Alabama anything for her birthday. Once Alabama entered into the foster care system, none of her foster-parents had cared enough to bother either.

"I'm not taking it back, Alabama. You need it. *I* need you to have it. I need to know you'll be safe when I'm not around."

Alabama looked around quickly, and seeing no one blurted, "I've never gotten a present before." Tears sprang into her eyes and she tried to blink them back.

"Hey, look at me, sweet." Abe couldn't believe what he'd just heard. He knew Alabama must've had a tough upbringing, but it'd obviously been worse than he'd imagined. When she wouldn't look up, he put his hand under her chin gently. "Please?"

Alabama finally looked up. She'd controlled her tears enough that they wouldn't fall, but tears were still pooled in her eyes. "Thank you, Christopher," she managed.

"You're welcome. You'll keep it?" Abe wanted to demand to know what had happened and how it was that she'd never been given a gift before, but he also didn't want to make her cry. He could see she was holding on by a thread.

At her nod he told her, "Okay then. When we get home tonight you can plug it in and charge it up. Be sure you take it with you wherever you go just in case you need it. I've loaded it up with five hundred minutes to get you started."

"That's too much," Alabama managed to get out.

"No, it's not. It's not enough for my peace of mind, but I knew you wouldn't accept it if I'd put as many minutes on there as I wanted to. Besides, you'll probably use all those up in the first week talking to me. At least I hope you might."

Alabama smiled. Jeez, he was amazing. "Okay. Thank you, Christopher. Seriously."

Abe didn't think, he just tipped Alabama's chin up higher with his finger, leaned in, and gave her a quick kiss on the corner of her mouth. He didn't linger, although he wanted to. The quick taste he'd gotten of her was enough to drive him crazy. Alabama tasted like peppermint, and he wanted more. Abe forced himself to drop his hand, caressing her chin before letting go, and then turning toward the steering wheel. He started the engine and headed out of the parking lot.

Alabama couldn't believe Christopher had just kissed her. It *did* count as a kiss right? It was short and sweet, but it was awesome. Much better than the sloppy French kisses she'd received in the past. She could still feel the touch of Christopher's fingers against her jaw. Alabama leaned back into the seat, trusting Christopher to get them wherever they were going safely. She looked down at the phone in her lap. He made her feel safe. She'd never felt that way before.

THE DAY HAD been awesome. Alabama didn't think she'd ever smiled so much in her entire life. Christopher had first driven them to the beach. Riverton was a suburb of San Diego and Alabama hadn't had a lot of time to spend at the beach. Alabama loved the water, but this was the first time she'd experienced a picnic in the sand. The beach wasn't one of the touristy ones. In fact she'd only seen a handful of people the entire time they'd been there.

Christopher had brought a light blanket and a thermos of coffee and some fruit. They'd sat on the beach and watched the water. They'd talked a bit, but mostly they'd just enjoyed the morning air and being in each other's company.

Next they'd gone to the San Diego zoo. Alabama generally didn't like zoos. She'd always felt sorry for the animals. She didn't think they were being abused in any way, but she just thought it was sad to see the majestic animals cooped up behind the bars of their cages. But Alabama wasn't thinking too much about that while visiting with Christopher.

He'd taken hold of her hand as they walked around and hadn't let go. When the crowds got bigger Christopher brought her to his side and protected her from being jostled by the other people rushing here and there. A man accidentally dropped his drink and it splashed onto her jeans and shoes. Alabama thought Christopher was going to lose it. When he looked like he was going to go after the man and beat the crap out of him, all Alabama had to do was put her hand on Christopher's arm and he'd stopped. She watched as he visibly controlled himself. It was fascinating.

Christopher kissed her hand and tucked her deeper into his side. He'd glared at the man as they walked by, but otherwise let it drop.

After spending most of the day at the zoo, and eating way too much junk food, he'd driven them to the end of an air strip near his base. Of course Christopher was able to get onto the base with his credentials. He'd parked the car and helped Alabama get out. Christopher spread the blanket they'd used on the beach on the trunk of his car, and they'd settled on it. They leaned back against the back window and watched the planes take off and land.

Abe interlaced their fingers together on one hand and brought them to rest against his belly. They'd talked softly about nothing in particular.

When it began to get dark, Christopher helped her off the car and back into the passenger seat. They'd picked up Chinese food to go and gone back to her apartment.

After eating dinner, they'd settled on the couch and Alabama put in *The Princess Bride* for background noise. She'd seen it so many times she'd memorized all the lines.

They'd been watching for about twenty minutes before Christopher broke the silence. "Tell me more about you, Alabama. Tell me about why you look around before you talk to me when we're in public, but at night, when you're here, in your own space, you become much more talkative. Is it only because no one is here to overhear you and judge you? Or is there more?"

Alabama tried to pull her hand away from his instinctively. Abe wouldn't let go, and instead pulled her toward him and into his side. He tucked her head into his chest and murmured "Shhhh sweet. You're safe here. Talk to me. Let me in."

It was crazy. She was seriously considering it. No one else had ever cared enough to notice or ask. Was she just feeling this way toward Christopher because she hadn't ever felt this way before? Or was it real? Alabama had no idea, but she wanted to try. She *wanted* to trust him.

"I…" she paused. Jesus. She couldn't do this.

Christopher didn't say anything, just continued to rub her arm up and down and rub his thumb over the back of her hand as it rested against him.

His silent support, along with the fact she didn't have to look at him while she told him her pathetic story, gave her the courage to continue.

"You're right. While it's true I'm not comfortable with others overhearing my thoughts when I talk to people…that's not the only reason. My mama wasn't…nice. She…she didn't want me, but for some reason didn't give me up for adoption. I wish she had."

"Jesus," Abe murmured. "Come here, sweet."

He shifted on the small couch until he was prone and Alabama was lying against him. The back of the couch was behind her and Christopher was half under her and half beside her. One arm was around her waist holding her close. The other arm was wrapped around her shoulders and tangled into her hair. He pressed her head to his chest. "Close your eyes, feel me here with you. You're safe. Tell me."

He was demanding, but Alabama didn't feel threatened. She'd never been held like this. She'd spent the night with a guy before, but as soon as he'd had sex with her, he'd rolled over and she waited a miserable six hours for the sun to rise so she could get out of his apartment.

Christopher was warm and smelled so good. She wasn't sure what he smelled like, just that it was comforting. She closed her eyes as he'd demanded and burrowed closer to him.

"Mama named me Alabama Ford Smith. Alabama because that's the state she got fucked in...her words, not mine...and Ford because that's *where* she got fucked. Her last name wasn't even Smith. She didn't want me to have her last name." Alabama gripped the sleeve of Christopher's shirt with her left hand without even realizing it and continued.

"My earliest memory is being locked in a closet and having Mama yell at me to shut up. I don't know why I was crying, but she couldn't stand it. Anytime I'd speak to her, she'd lock me in the closet. I learned not to talk to her if I wanted to eat or even sleep in my bed. But sometimes I'd forget. Or I'd talk not knowing she was around to hear me. I still hear her yelling at me to shut up over and over again."

Abe wanted to tell Alabama to stop, that he couldn't bear it, but he knew she had to get it out. He couldn't believe she was as sweet as she was. Other people who'd gone through what she had wouldn't have turned out half as adjusted as Alabama was, and he knew she was probably downplaying it anyway. Even knowing her for the short time he had, he knew she wouldn't tell him everything.

"When I was eleven, she hit me with a skillet because I'd asked her something. A teacher noticed and I trusted a police officer when he said he'd help me. He didn't, and they sent me back to her. When I was twelve, she beat me with that same skillet and broke my jaw, along with most of my face. She swore, as she was hitting me, that she'd teach me not to talk."

Alabama stopped and cleared her throat. She'd never talked so much at one time in all her life. But it felt good to get it out. To tell someone. To tell Christopher. She finally noticed Christopher's hand clenched in a fist at her side. He'd bunched up her shirt and was holding it tight. She lifted her head and brought her hand up to his face.

"Are you all right?"

Abe snorted. Of course she'd try to comfort *him*. *He* should be comforting *her*. He tried to relax; unclenching his fist and soothing it over her side. "I'm okay, sweet. I'm just pissed as hell at your mother and trying to understand how you turned out to be the sweetest woman I've ever met with your upbringing."

Alabama just shook her head and put her head back on his chest.

Abe didn't make her look up at him, but told her quietly, "Seriously, sweet. You don't have to say a word and your goodness comes through loud and clear. I could sense it standing at that damn table at the party." When she didn't say anything else Abe decided not to push. "What then? Where did you go after she beat you?"

"Into foster care."

"Was it...okay?"

"I guess. Mama had told me to shut up so many times in my life I'd finally taken her words to heart. Everyone thought I was weird and I didn't talk to many people. Even today when I hear the words 'shut up,' I cringe. It brings me back to sitting in that damn closet and listening to my mama screaming at me to 'shut up, shut up, shut up.' You said something to me once and I think you were right."

"What's that?"

"You said I had Posttraumatic Stress Disorder. I hadn't thought of it that way, but you're probably right. I think I need to talk to someone about it. I mean...other than you."

"I'll help you with whatever you need. If you want me to help you find someone, let me know. There are lots of counselors on base that have experience with PTSD. If you'd prefer to talk to someone who specifically deals with child abuse, I can help with that too. But sweet, you'll never know how much it means to me that you trusted me with your story. I know we're still getting to know each other, but you mean something to me. I won't let you down. I won't tell you to 'shut up' now that I know it's a trigger for you. I've told you this before, and I'll keep saying it, you're safe with me. I promise.

"Also, your mother might have tried to give you a

name that didn't mean anything, but you should own it. You *are* Alabama Ford Smith. You've survived. You've persevered. Don't let her own petty actions stain you. Those are *her* issues, not yours. You're unique and amazing and you have a unique and amazing name. Besides, I *like* your name. I like you."

Alabama turned her face into Christopher's shirt and inhaled deeply. God, he was awesome. She tried not to cry, but it was no use. The tears came out of her eyes and leaked down onto his chest when she turned her head back to the side so she could breathe.

"Let it out sweet. Let it out. I'm here. I'm not going anywhere."

Alabama cried for her lousy childhood. She cried because her mama had never loved her. She cried for her loss of trust in people in general. Finally when she was all cried out, she sniffed once and settled on Christopher's chest. She relaxed into him, thinking how comfortable she was and she never wanted to move.

Abe was furious. He tried to stay relaxed under Alabama, but he didn't know how successful he was at it. He decided to share some of his life with Alabama, so she didn't feel awkward about sharing something so intimate about herself with him.

"I didn't really know my dad growing up." Abe felt Alabama's head lift as she looked at him, but he kept talking. "He would come around every now and then, but just as we were used to him being around, he'd leave again. My mom would cry every time he left. She never knew I knew about it, but I'd sit outside her bedroom and listen to her bawl her eyes out. I swore I'd take care of her. I did what I could. I did my chores without being asked, I helped my sisters with their homework, and I gave my mom every cent I earned from mowing lawns and other small jobs I did for the neighbors."

Abe stroked Alabama's hair, not sure if he was comforting her or himself. "We didn't have a lot of money, because my dad certainly didn't contribute, but we did okay. I'd do anything for my sisters and mother, and it hurts me that you didn't have that in your life. I wish I'd known you when you were growing up, Alabama."

Alabama didn't say a word, but lay in Christopher's arms, loving the feel of his arms around her. She thought about what he'd just told her about his family. Alabama understood more about what made him how he was today. "You need to take care of people," she told him drowsily.

"I take care of those that mean something to me."

Alabama didn't say anything else, but his words settled into her soul and she could almost feel the crack in her heart healing.

Abe continued to run his hand over Alabama's hair until she finally fell asleep on his chest.

He'd never wanted to hurt a woman before, but Abe

wanted to hurt Alabama's mother more than he'd ever wanted anything before in his life. How could she do that to her own child? How could she take someone as sweet as Alabama and abuse her that way? He was amazed she'd turned out as well as she had. It said a lot about Alabama's inner strength.

Abe lay under Alabama enjoying her softness, enjoying her trust in him. He'd never forget this moment. It was the moment he knew he could easily fall head over heels in love with a woman for the first time in his life.

Chapter Nine

A LABAMA OPENED THE door to the temporary offices of Wolfe Realty. The building was much like the old one. The offices were all on one floor, but this time the realtors had to share offices until the new building was constructed.

It was actually easier to clean this building than the old one because everything had been destroyed in the fire and there wasn't as much clutter around.

Alabama pushed her new cleaning cart as she moved through the building. She'd always loved the quiet of the evening when she'd worked. Some people didn't like empty buildings and thought they were creepy, not Alabama. She loved the solitude.

She thought back over the last week. She and Christopher had spent every evening together. He had to work during the days, but had come over each night for dinner before she headed to work and to spend time with her.

One evening when she'd had the night off, they'd

gone to his quarters on the base. They weren't anything special, but to Alabama it was a whole new world. She didn't know anything about the military, and in fact being on the base itself made her nervous. There were unwritten rules she had no idea about. In order to get inside the grocery store you had to prove you were affiliated with the military and you had to show your identification. The same was true of a lot of the services on the base. It wasn't that anyone was unfriendly, it was just overwhelming.

Christopher sensed her unease and hadn't asked if she wanted to come to his place on base after the first time they'd been there, telling her since she was more comfortable at her apartment, he'd come to her. He hadn't seemed unhappy about it, simply telling her it wasn't a big deal.

Alabama loved hanging out with him. It was easy. It wasn't until the third evening they'd spent some time together that Christopher had asked if he could kiss her.

Alabama stood in the hallway of the building she was cleaning and closed her eyes recalling how perfect that first kiss was. They'd been sitting on her small couch watching some movie when she'd felt him looking at her. She turned to him and the look on his face was intense. When their eyes met his hand came up and cupped her cheek. She tilted her head and rested her cheek into his hand.

"I want to kiss you, sweet. Will you let me?"

Alabama simply nodded.

The hand at her cheek shifted to the back of her neck. Christopher cupped her in a firm, but strangely gentle grip, and shifted closer to her. He'd rested his forehead against hers and just held her there for a moment.

"I've been wanting to do this since you opened your door to me last week. You have no idea…"

Then he brought his other hand up to her face and cupped it. Alabama was sandwiched between the hand at the back of her neck and the one on her face. She didn't feel trapped, she felt protected. Christopher tilted her head just so and swooped in for his kiss. For some reason, Alabama had thought he'd take it slow. Everything he'd done so far had been easy and gentle, but this kiss wasn't either of those.

It was a confident kiss, a kiss that demanded she open and let him in. And she did. Alabama didn't hold back. Their lips met and immediately parted. She felt his tongue do an initial sweep of her mouth, then retreat to tease and caress her lips before plunging back in. Alabama tried to keep up, swirling her tongue around his, and at one point taking his tongue and sucking on it. She thought she'd feel awkward and uneasy, but she'd been so aroused, she didn't have time to be embarrassed.

At that point, Christopher took the hand that had

been on her cheek and put it on her back and laid her down against the cushions of the couch. He kept his hand at her neck supporting her head as he eased her down. Alabama didn't even notice…until she felt his hardness against her. Christopher never stopped his sensual exploration of her mouth, but she could feel his strength over her. He wasn't crushing her, in fact, his body felt good pressing against hers. She could feel his length against her leg—he was hard, all over.

Alabama breathed in through her nose and pressed her head back, breaking contact with his lips. Without missing a beat, Christopher leaned down and put his mouth against her neck, nipping and sucking lightly. Her breath came out in pants and she tried to get her brain to start working again.

"Now *that* was a kiss," she'd said breathlessly. She heard him chuckle against her throat before he moved up and nipped her earlobe.

"You make me lose my mind, sweet."

One part of Alabama wanted to do nothing more than stand up and lead him to her small bed in the corner, but the other part of her was terrified. She'd trusted before and been let down. She didn't think Christopher would break her trust, but she wasn't certain yet.

Alabama brought her hands down from his back where she'd been clutching at him and put them on his chest. He'd immediately reared up so he could see her face. Of course that pushed his erection harder into her thigh, making her blush. Christopher laughed and kissed her lightly on the nose. He sat them both up and brought her into his side.

"Thank you, Alabama. That was the best kiss I've ever had."

They hadn't said much more that night, they'd simply finished the movie. When it was over and time for Christopher to leave, she'd walked him to her door and he'd taken both of her hands in his and held them loosely in between them. Christopher leaned forward and touched his lips to hers. What started out as a short, sweet goodnight kiss turned into something hotter and longer.

He hadn't let go of her hands while they were kissing and it was interesting to be touching him with nothing more than her lips and tongue. Just that contact made her squirm. She'd never felt anything like she did when she was with him...kissing him.

"Good night, sweet. Lock the door behind me," was all he'd said. Then he'd kissed her once more on the tip of her nose, squeezed her hands, and walked out.

Alabama took a deep breath and opened her eyes. She'd zoned out in the middle of the hallway of the realty office. She'd been clenching the handles of the cleaning cart so hard, her fingernails had bit into her palms. She had it bad.

She laughed at herself and continued down the hall. Alabama had just entered one of the agent's offices when she heard the front door open. It wasn't too late, but late enough that there really shouldn't be anyone working. Feeling her heart jump with fear, Alabama stood stock still, not knowing what she should do. She reached in her pocket for the phone Christopher had given her, feeling better knowing she had some sort of way to call for help. She pulled it out and flipped it open. She pushed a nine and a one and her thumb hovered over the last one. She'd wait to see what was going on before she actually dialed for emergency help.

She watched down the hall and soon she saw someone walking toward her. It was Adelaide. Alabama let out a breath of relief. She didn't want to see the woman, but at least it wasn't a crazed killer. She shut the phone and slipped it back into her pocket.

Adelaide looked up when she was a few doors down from Alabama and finally noticed her.

"What are you doing here?" She asked nastily.

Alabama thought it was a pretty dumb question considering she was the janitor and was standing in front of a cleaning cart. She gestured toward the cart and didn't answer verbally.

"Yeah, I forgot you don't talk much do you?" Adelaide sneered. "I came in to get some papers for a client that I left here by accident. Get out of my way."

Alabama moved to the side and watched as Adelaide brushed past her into the office she'd been about to clean.

"By the way, I know all about you and Abe, bitch. He was mine and you stole him. But don't worry; he'll come back to me. After all, look at *you*, then look at *me*. There's no way he's serious about you. You're short and plain. You can't hold his attention for a millisecond."

Alabama had enough. At no time had Christopher made her feel as if he was playing with her or just clocking time. He'd mentioned to her several times that he hadn't been serious with Adelaide. She was just being mean and jealous and taking it out on her.

Alabama looked around, still not being able to break the habit, and responded quietly and firmly, "I didn't steal anything. *He* came to *me*. I might not be as pretty as you, but it doesn't seem to matter to him. He likes me, and I like him. So back off and leave us alone."

As far as comebacks go, it was pretty lame, but Adelaide actually took a step back in surprise. She hadn't expected the meek little janitor to fight back. Maybe no one had ever talked back to her, although that was unlikely. It seemed Adelaide was the kind of woman who'd make enemies, and surely someone had protested being talked down to.

Adelaide narrowed her eyes and glared at Alabama.

Alabama glared right back.

"You'll regret this, bitch," Adelaide finally hissed. She turned toward the desk and grabbed a folder that was sitting on it. "And get out of my office. I don't trust you to keep your hands off my stuff."

That hurt Alabama more than Adelaide's previous words had. She might not be the prettiest person in the world, but she wasn't a thief. Even at her lowest, when she'd turned eighteen and had gotten free of the foster care system, she hadn't resorted to shoplifting. There were times she would've killed to have something to eat other than cheap noodles, but she'd never taken something that wasn't hers.

Without looking behind her, Alabama pushed her cart down the hall. Fine, if Adelaide didn't want her office cleaned, she wouldn't bother. Hopefully the spiders and dust took over the space and made Adelaide miserable.

Alabama entered the office next to Adelaide's and heard the bitch stomp down the hall and exit the building. Once Adelaide left, Alabama sat down wearily on the chair next to the desk. Damn. She didn't like confrontations, but she felt good for finally sticking up for herself for once. Adelaide was a bitch, but luckily she didn't have to work with her. Hopefully she'd remember her papers from here on out and Alabama could avoid another nasty encounter with her.

Chapter Ten

THE NEXT COUPLE of weeks were some of the best in Alabama's life. She'd been spending a lot of time with Christopher and tonight they were going to go out with his SEAL teammates and their girlfriends.

Alabama was beyond nervous. She wasn't good in crowds, especially out in public, but she wanted to do this for Christopher. He'd been so good to her. He hadn't pushed her to have sex, even though it was obvious he was ready. They'd had a few serious make out sessions on her couch and she knew it'd been hard for him to stop. Hell, it'd been hard for *her* to stop.

The last one ended with both of them with their shirts off and he'd actually made her explode with just his lips on her breasts. She'd never experienced that kind of passion before and it had freaked her out. Christopher had immediately noticed, and instead of pressuring her to continue, he soothed her. He pulled her into his chest and just held her. He'd been so good to her. She knew she was in way over her head with him. Alabama was pretty sure she loved Christopher. She wasn't sure she really knew what love was, but not a minute went by during the day that she didn't want to talk to him, to see him, to spend time with him.

The first time she'd called him on her new mobile phone, Christopher had been so happy. He didn't try to hide his excitement and joy that she'd actually called him. When he'd calmed down to find out what she needed, he was speechless for a moment when she'd told him she'd just wanted to say hi.

So tonight they were going to a local bar, called *Aces Bar and Grill*, that apparently catered to military members, especially SEALs. Alabama had heard a lot about Matthew, also known as Wolf, and his girlfriend, Caroline. But apparently there were four others on the team that were like brothers to Christopher. There was Sam, whose nickname was Mozart, Hunter, whose nickname was Cookie, Kason went by Benny, and finally Faulkner who they called Dude.

There was no way she'd remember everyone's name, but she'd try to go with the flow. Christopher had promised to help her. When Alabama asked about the team's nicknames and their history, he'd only chuckled and told her that it was up to each man to explain it, if they so choose.

She shrugged. That was the least of her worries.

Alabama clutched Christopher's hand, desperately,

as they headed toward the entrance of *Aces*. Before they went inside, Christopher stopped and pulled her to the side of the door and backed her against the wall.

Christopher bought his hand up to her face and cupped her cheek. He did that a lot when he wanted her to look into his eyes while he spoke to her. It should irritate Alabama, but it didn't. It made her feel warm inside. She loved his hands on her.

"It's going to be fine, sweet. I'll be right there with you. You'll be safe. They'll like you, I promise."

At her nod, he held her eyes for a moment then leaned forward and brushed his lips over her eyebrows, then her nose, then finally her lips. He didn't linger, but nipped her bottom lip gently once, and drew back. "You're the bravest person I've ever met. Come on; let's go in before you have a heart attack."

Alabama could feel her heart beating double time in her chest. She was nervous, but having Christopher there helped. She wanted his friends to like her, but she didn't really know how to make friends. She wasn't good at it.

They walked toward a large table in the back of the room. There were a group of people already seated and laughing together.

There was a pretty waitress standing at the table taking drink orders. She was about normal height and was wearing a pair of sneakers, unlike the other waitresses who were all wearing high heels. She also stood out from the other servers in the bar because she was wearing a modest tank top and a pair of jeans, instead of a skimpy shirt and a mini-skirt. Her attire did nothing to distract from how pretty she was.

She had long black hair which was pulled back into a braid that ended midway down her back. She finished up taking everyone's drink order as they arrived at the table.

"Hey! You got here just in time, what can I get you from the bar?"

The nametag on the waitress' tag read, 'Jess.'

Abe turned to Alabama and gestured for her to order.

"Coke please," Alabama said softly.

Christopher squeezed her hand to reassure her and Alabama tried to relax. "Hey, Jess. I'll take whatever you have on tap tonight." It was obvious Christopher knew the waitress, probably because the group of friends came to the bar frequently.

"No problem. I'll be back soon," Jess said in a confident voice.

Alabama watched as the waitress limped away from the table. She had just a second to wonder what was wrong with the pretty waitress before Christopher put his hand on the small of her back and turned her to the table.

Alabama looked up to see that everyone was looking at them. She gripped Christopher's hand as if it was the only thing keeping her above water.

"Hey guys," Abe said easily. "This is Alabama. She's nervous to meet all of you, so go easy all right?" He said it lightly, but there was steel running through his words.

He'd had a talk with his team that day and they all knew how shy Alabama was, just as they knew how important she was to Abe. Abe had also told them a little of her childhood and they'd all been taken aback. They all knew such abuses happened all the time, but they hated it'd happened to someone who was so obviously important to their teammate.

Finding a good woman was new to the team. They'd all been there when Caroline had almost died at the hands of terrorists and had seen how hard Wolf had struggled to finally get the nerve to claim her.

None of them would admit it, but they were all a bit jealous. Seeing the close relationship they shared had finally brought home to them all how meaningless their one night stands were. They were all itching to find someone for their own, and it looked like Abe just might be the next in line to find a woman for himself.

Tamping down the impulse to look around the room, Alabama gripped Christopher's hand so hard she knew he'd have indentations from her fingernails, and simply said, "Hi."

"Hey, Alabama, glad you could make it," said a gorgeous man who'd stood as they'd arrived. The other men also added their greetings and Christopher led her to a seat at the end of the table against the wall. He waited until she was seated and then settled next to her. He put his arm on the back of her chair and leaned in.

"Okay, sweet?"

Alabama looked at Christopher and nodded. He really was a good guy. She vaguely noticed how all the men were seated in such a way that they could see the rest of the room. Obviously they all felt the same way Christopher did about putting their back to a room.

"I guess we should all introduce ourselves," a beautiful woman sitting in the middle of the table said in Alabama's direction. "Don't worry, if you don't remember everyone's names. It took me forever to remember them myself!"

Everyone around the table laughed.

"And I'll do it, 'cos if the guys do it you'll only hear their nicknames and you'll never learn their real names. I'm trying to get them to use their given names, but they're hopeless! I'm Caroline and I'm with this big lug, Matthew. Sitting at the end is Sam and his girlfriend Molly. Next to them is Faulkner and Brittany. Then there's Kason and Emily, and finally, across from you, is Hunter and Michele."

When she'd introduced them, everyone said hello at

once and then started talking again. Alabama breathed a sigh of relief that no one seemed to want to draw her into conversation yet.

Alabama listened as the men joked with one another. It was tough to keep everyone straight, especially when the men called each other by their nicknames and the women used their real names. It was if there were double the number of people sitting at the table.

"Hey, Christopher, how did you guys meet?" Alabama thought it was Kason's girlfriend that had asked, but she couldn't remember her name.

"Remember that fire a month or so ago?" Christopher asked. When the women all nodded he continued. "Alabama saved my life. She was there and helped get me and a bunch of other people out of the building."

"Whoa, that's intense," Michele said. "Didn't you go to that party with Adelaide?"

Abe's eyes squinted like they did when he was pissed. Alabama didn't know what was up with Michele and her attitude, but it obviously pissed Christopher off.

"Yeah, I did, but it didn't work out. I met Alabama that night and things went from there."

Michele obviously didn't know when to stop, because she continued, "What did Adelaide have to say about that?"

Cookie didn't give Christopher time to respond because he jumped in. "What the hell Michele? Abe's with

Alabama now, give it a rest."

Alabama was confused and freaked out. She'd never met Michele, but it seemed as if she didn't like her…at all.

"We all know you and Adelaide are tight, but Jesus, woman, Abe dumped her because she was acting crazy. I told you to let it drop and here you are bringing it up in front of his new woman." Cookie was obviously pissed. Strangely enough him being pissed seemed to calm Abe down.

"Let's go," Cookie told the woman at his side. "We're done. Abe man, sorry. Alabama, it was nice meeting you. You're way too good for an asshole like Abe here, but damn glad you're overlooking that. Hope to see you again soon." With that, Cookie forced Michele up with a hand on her elbow and without giving her a chance to say anything, led her away from the group.

Alabama didn't know what to say, so she just sat there embarrassed.

"Jesus, sorry about that Abe, Alabama," Benny said softly, leaning across the table toward his teammate and his date. "Alabama, he's been seeing Michele for a while. She and Adelaide are friends. Obviously it was a mistake to bring her tonight."

Abe nodded stiffly. Jesus, he'd wanted to make sure Alabama would meet his friends in as stress-free of an environment as possible, and Cookie's girl-of-the-month had to go and ruin it. He looked down at Alabama.

Feeling Christopher's eyes on her, Alabama looked up. He looked tense and pissed on her behalf. She giggled a small quiet giggle and watched as his eyebrows rose questionably.

Alabama knew she had to grow a backbone. The whole thing was pretty funny if she thought about it. She wanted to reassure Christopher that she was all right. She didn't want him to think she'd cry every time some woman brought her claws out. Hell, with the way he looked, she'd be crying all the time. She knew every woman in the place was jealous as hell of her, and it strangely cheered her up.

Not being able to stop her eyes from scanning the interior of the bar before reassuring Christopher she paused, then leaned up toward him and whispered in his ear teasingly, "Any other friends of your ex-girlfriend I have to worry about tonight?"

She pulled back and smiled at him, making sure he knew she was teasing him. She watched as his eyelids fell and his pupils dilated. "Shit, Alabama, I was worried you'd be freaked."

Not breaking eye contact she told him quietly, "I *am* a little freaked, but you're here with *me*, not her. Hunter didn't let her stay, and I like your friends. I'm determined not to let it bother me."

Abe let out the breath he'd been holding. He'd been ready to escort Michele out himself. Damn her. She'd brought up Adelaide purposely, just to be catty. He hoped Cookie wouldn't be seeing her anymore. Anyone that deliberately set out to hurt someone else wasn't someone anyone on the team wanted to be around.

Before Abe could pull Alabama into his arms and kiss the hell out of her, Emily piped up, "So, Abe huh? I've heard the stories about the others, but what's the story of your nickname?"

Normally the guys would leave it up to their friends to explain their own names, but Dude jumped in before Abe could say anything.

"Abe, like Honest Abe," he explained. "There was this one time in BUD/S when this one loser decided he was too tired to clean his own shit, and in the middle of the night swapped it with Abe's gear. Dumbass didn't realize the gear had serial numbers on it. So in the morning when inspection was going on and Abe saw his gear wasn't his own, he went on a mission to find out who'd swapped it. Didn't take long. Abe made sure to teach him a lesson he wouldn't forget. Asshole rang out that morning."

There was a lot about the story Alabama didn't really understand, but she nodded as if she did.

Dude continued the explanation. "Ever since then anytime anyone stepped out of line and tried to get out of something by lying or stealing, Abe called 'em on it. The name stuck."

Abe revealed more when he continued. "I can't stand it when people lie or steal. There's just no need for it. We've seen some crazy shit on missions. People in poor countries stealing food from women and kids. People lying their asses off just to get an extra cup of water or bread. On one hand, I know desperation makes people do things they might not otherwise do, but it sticks in my craw every time. I hate it. I'd rather people be honest and upfront about what they need or want them to lie about it."

Benny jumped into the conversation agreeing. "Yeah, remember that one chick you…er…dated that was wearing that smokin' hot dress, but when you got her home you found she still had the tag on it? She was gonna bring it back to the store and get her money back after wearing it…"

He stopped because Caroline had smacked his arm, hard. "Jeez, Kason, have some class. You can't talk about previous uh…girlfriends when his current girlfriend is sitting right next to him!"

Looking confused, Benny sputtered, "What?"

Alabama giggled again and looked at Christopher. He just shook his head and murmured, "Jesus, this was a bad idea." Alabama laughed at him again and put her hand on his thigh.

Loving the feel of Alabama's hand on his leg, Abe put his hand over hers and intertwined their fingers. He then tried to clarify what his friends were bungling so badly. "What my so-called 'friends' here are trying to say is, that I don't like liars, and I don't like people who steal. Even buying a dress with the intention of wearing it and then returning it is a type of stealing. It's not right and it's not cool."

Alabama got what he was saying and gripped his thigh harder, making him look down at her. "I don't lie or steal."

Abe smiled. "I know, sweet. You're too nice to do either."

The night continued and Alabama relaxed. She was actually having a good time and no one seemed concerned she wasn't talking much. At one point, when she'd stood up to go to the restroom, Caroline joined her. "You know us women can't go by ourselves. We'll be back," she'd exclaimed to the group at large.

Then she'd taken Alabama's hand and they'd walked toward the restroom. Upon arriving they'd done their business and when they were washing their hands, Caroline said what she'd obviously been wanting to say all night.

"Christopher's a good man. He was on the plane with me, Matthew, and Sam when the terrorists tried to take it down. He was the one who gave me my nickname. He was the one who convinced Matthew to fight for me. I'd do anything for him. *Anything.*"

Alabama flinched. Here it came. Caroline obviously didn't think she was good enough for Christopher.

"That being said, I like you. You're just what he needs. I've never seen Christopher so relaxed. The way he looks at you is how Matthew looks at me. If you're just using him for whatever reason, please let him go now. But if you really like him, and I think you do, please protect his heart. These guys are tough. They're strong and macho, but they're marshmallows inside. You can hurt him. I'm just asking you not to."

Taking a quick glance around the empty bathroom, Alabama forced herself to answer and to try to reassure the other woman. "I'm not going to hurt Christopher. I like him. I know I'm not good enough for him, but until he figures that out, I'm staying."

The smile that came across Caroline's face was blinding. She reached out and pulled Alabama into a hug. Alabama was too surprised to do anything other than awkwardly put her arms around the other woman.

"Welcome to the family, Alabama," Caroline gushed. "I'm so glad Christopher has found someone who's worthy of him. Not some skank who just wants in his pants."

Alabama did something she'd never done in her life before, she blurted out, without thinking, without looking around to make sure Mama wasn't lingering nearby, "Oh, I want in his pants all right."

Caroline pulled back in surprise, then leaned back and laughed as if Alabama had just said the funniest thing she'd ever heard. "Oh man, you guys haven't done it yet?"

Embarrassed now, Alabama could only shake her head.

"Now I know he *really* likes you. Hang on tight, girlfriend. Hang on for the ride of your life. If you ever need me, don't hesitate to contact me. Us old ladies have to stick together."

Alabama could only nod as Caroline grabbed her hand again and they walked back toward the table.

When they arrived, Caroline gave her another secret smile and sat down next to her man. Alabama watched as Matthew leaned toward Caroline and kissed her. It wasn't a polite "I'm-in-front-of-company" kiss either. It was passionate, and it lingered. Alabama was almost embarrassed to be a witness to it. But on the other hand it was amazing. It was the kiss a man gave to his woman. A kiss that showed her how much he loved her, how much he couldn't wait to get her alone. It was beautiful.

Looking away, Alabama caught Christopher's eye. Whoa. His eyes bored into hers. "Everything go okay in the restroom? She didn't scare you away?"

Alabama shook her head. "No, she was great actually. You have amazing friends."

"I do, don't I?" He paused. "You ready to go?"

"Go? But it's still early…"

"I want to be alone with you. I want you, Alabama."

Alabama's stomach did flip flops. Did she want this? If they left now, she knew they'd end up in bed together. She didn't want to overanalyze it. "I want you too."

At her words Abe's breathing sped up. He put his hand on her elbow and immediately stood up. "It's been real guys, we're headed out. See ya later."

Without giving her a chance to say much more, he threw some bills on the table to cover their drinks and headed for the door.

Alabama looked back at the table to see Caroline wink at her. She smiled back.

THE RIDE BACK to Alabama's apartment was done mostly in silence. Alabama had told Christopher she'd been glad to meet his friends and he'd only grunted in response. Alabama almost laughed. It seemed as if their roles were reversed—he was the one without the verbal ability at the moment.

He drove quickly, but safely, through the streets back to her little apartment. Alabama knew what was coming and was nervous, but excited. It was time. She was ready to make love to Christopher.

Christopher parked his car and silently got out and met her at the front of the car. Alabama was too impatient to wait for him to come and get her out of the car. They walked hand in hand up the stairs to her apartment. Alabama handed over her keys when they reached her door and he unlocked it for them. Christopher placed the keys in a basket by the door and slipped her purse off her shoulder. He took her face into his hands and leaned down to kiss her.

Abe was holding on by a slender thread. Alabama was sexy as hell and he couldn't wait to get inside her. She was everything he'd ever wanted in a woman. She was sweet and kind and beautiful. He kissed Alabama deeply while walking her backwards into the room. He hadn't dared pay any attention to her small bed in the corner before. He knew he wanted her there, but he'd been taking things slow. They were finally ready.

He backed her toward the bed until her knees touched the mattress. Abe wanted nothing more than to push her back on the bed and strip her naked, but he had to make sure she was on the same page as he was. "You want this right, sweet? It's not just me?"

"Make love to me, Christopher. I'm yours."

Abe didn't hesitate. Alabama's words were all the permission he hadn't known he'd been waiting for. He grasped her shirt at the hem and drew it upward, not breaking eye contact. He wanted Alabama to know he saw *her*. That he wasn't stripping just another woman's body, but he was stripping *his* woman's body.

Alabama's heart skipped a beat as she watched Christopher's eyes as he drew her shirt up and off. It wasn't until he threw it behind him on the floor that he took his eyes from her face and ran them down her body. Of course, he'd seen her before in their make out sessions, but this was different. This was more intimate, more personal. More everything.

"God, sweet. You. Are. Beautiful."

Abe took Alabama's hands in his and held them out away from her body. She *was* beautiful. Her bra was a basic black cotton piece, but it fit her personality. The dark fabric against her light skin made for a wonderful contrast. "Take if off for me," he murmured letting go of her hands so she could obey him.

Alabama blushed, but did as he asked without question. Whatever he wanted, she'd do. She reached behind her and unclasped the hooks of her bra. She dropped her arms and the straps fell down her shoulders and then down and off her arms. She caught the garment with her hand and let it drop to the floor.

Abe inhaled. He wasn't going to last long. She was perfect. He watched as her nipples beaded as he took her in. She was breathing hard, but he could tell it wasn't in fear. Alabama wanted him as much as he wanted her.

He took her hands in his again and once again held

them out to her sides. "Beautiful," he murmured as he leaned forward and took one of her pouty nipples into his mouth.

Alabama groaned. Abe knew how sensitive her breasts were from their earlier sessions on the couch. She tugged at her hands, wanting to touch him. Wanting to make him feel as good as he was making her feel. Abe didn't let go, and instead tightened his hold on her. She'd do as Abe wanted, if he let her do what *she* wanted, he'd never last.

Abe knew he was on the edge. He couldn't wait anymore. This first time was going to be quick, but he consoled himself with the thought that they had all night.

He finally dropped her hands and reached for his own shirt. "Get undressed and get on the bed. I can't wait." His voice was low and hard, and sexy as hell.

Alabama watched as Christopher tore off his own shirt and bent down to undo his boots. She quickly unbuttoned her own jeans and shimmied out of them. She peeled her undies off and dove under the covers.

She watched as Christopher stood up and toed off his boots. He undid the buttons on his cargo pants and quickly shed them. Looking her in the eyes for the first time since they'd started undressing, he asked, "You ready for me?"

God yes, she'd been ready for him for a while now.

"Yes, I want to see you. Please."

Alabama inhaled as Christopher took off his boxer briefs. He was beautiful. He was larger than the only other man she'd slept with. She knew she didn't have a lot to compare him to, but he was long and obviously hard...for her. It was difficult for her to wrap her mind around everything that was finally happening between the two of them.

Before she'd gotten her fill of looking at him, Christopher threw back the covers and joined her.

"Don't hide from me. I want to see every inch of your delicious body."

He crushed her to him and growled into her mouth. He wanted to take his time and learn Alabama's body, but he couldn't, not this first time.

While kissing her, Abe brushed his hand down her body. Alabama moaned under him and opened her legs to him. Feeling she was just as excited as he was, Abe separated their lips by a scant inch and murmured, "You're so ready for me. I love feeling how wet you are, and it's all for me, isn't it?"

Alabama nodded and thrust her hips up into his hand as he caressed her deeper. "I'm ready. Please, Christopher."

Possessiveness shot through him unexpectedly. He never felt possessive toward any of the women he'd been with in the past. He guessed he'd been using them to get off just as they'd used him for the same. But with Alabama, it was different. She was his.

"This is gonna be quick. I had plans to take this slow. To make sure I memorized every inch of your body before making love to you, but I'm not gonna last. I'll make it up to you later. I can't wait. You're mine."

Alabama just nodded and gripped his biceps harder.

"Say it, Alabama. Mine."

Alabama gasped. "Yours, Christopher. Please."

"Are you protected sweet? I'm clean. I have to get tested by the Navy regularly."

Alabama tried to get her thoughts together. They should've had this talk already, but neither of them had been able to wait and she'd been too embarrassed to bring it up before.

"I'm on the pill. I needed to regulate my…er…you know."

Abe thought she was cute. She was embarrassed to talk about her period, but they were in bed about to do the most intimate thing two people could do with each other. Adorable.

Alabama continued, embarrassed. "And…uh…I'm clean too…I've only been with one other guy and it was a while ago…so…uh…"

"Shhhh, I know you are. I never thought differently. I want to come in you bare. But it's your choice. Whatever you want, it's up to you."

"You, I want *you*, Christopher, please," Alabama begged. She'd never felt this way before. The last time she'd slept with a guy, he'd barely gotten her wet and then shoved himself in. It had hurt, and he didn't seem to care. He just grunted and pumped in and out of her until he'd gotten off. Then he'd had the nerve to ask if it'd been as good for her as it had been for him. Thank God, she'd made him wear a condom.

She hadn't known how good sex could really be. Hell, she and Christopher hadn't had much foreplay either, but she was ready for him. More than ready. She was soaked. One kiss was all it took for her to want him more than her next breath.

Then he was there. Christopher eased up on his knees and looked down at Alabama. She lay before him naked with her skin gleaming from the sweat popping over her body. He ran his hands from her shoulders down to her belly and then up again. Squeezing and caressing. Up and down he went. "Beautiful," he exclaimed breathlessly. "Mine."

Alabama could only nod and watch as he spread her legs wider and scooted closer to her core. He raised her up until her ass was propped up and resting on his knees. He took hold of himself with one hand and placed the other on her pubis, right above where she wanted him most. He held her still as he slowly pushed the head of his cock into her tight center.

They both hissed at the pleasure.

"Please, Christopher, more."

Abe eased more of himself into her until his hips met hers. He put both hands on her hips and hauled her higher up on his thighs until they were fused together as close as two people could be. Abe leaned over her then and put his hands on the mattress next to her shoulders. "Hold on to me." He ordered hoarsely.

Alabama reached up and grabbed hold of his biceps again. She loved the way they flexed and moved with him. She couldn't reach all the way around them, and it made her feel tiny and small under him. She wrapped her legs around his hips and urged him on. "Please," was all she could get out.

Abe moved. God, she was hot and wet and all his. He looked down and saw Alabama had her head thrown back and her eyes were closed. "Look at me," he demanded. "Open your eyes and see who it is that's making love to you."

Alabama's eyes popped open at his request. Christopher was looking straight at her intensely. She gasped as he thrust harder.

"That's it. Look at me and know it's *me* that's here with you. You're mine. I'm not letting you go."

Alabama said the first thing that popped into her head. "Promise?"

"I promise. You're not going anywhere. Hell, I'm

not going anywhere."

Alabama kept her eyes on Christopher as he loved her. Time seemed to stand still and at the same time, fly by.

Abe watched as Alabama eased closer and closer to the edge. He brought one of his hands down to where they were joined and pressed, hard, right on her clit. That was just what she needed to fly over the edge. At his demand, she kept her eyes on his until the last minute, then she arched her back and thrust her hips into his harder and groaned his name.

That was all it took for Abe to lose it as well. He thrust into her one last time and held still as he emptied himself into her soft core.

After a minute or so, Abe took a deep breath and eased down next to Alabama, not leaving her. He loved the feel of her aftershocks clutching his body and wanted to keep that connection with her as long as he could.

Alabama was sprawled under him as if she was a rag doll. He'd ridden her hard, but she'd taken everything he'd given her. He couldn't hold his words back if his life depended on it.

"I love you."

Alabama's eyes popped open. It would've been comical if they were in any other position than what they were. Alabama couldn't believe what she'd just heard.

She had to have heard him wrong.

She closed her eyes, enjoying the feel of being still intimately joined with Christopher, and sighed happily. She had no idea. None. No wonder sex was so popular in books and movies if it felt like this.

"Did you hear me, sweet? I love you." Abe said it again, enjoying the clenching of her inner muscles at his words.

Alabama opened her eyes again and looked up at the gorgeous man hovering over her. He traced one eyebrow with his finger. "You're everything I've been looking for in a woman. I know it's been fast with us, but it's real. I know it. I won't let you go. You're mine. You admitted it. I'm not letting you renege on that."

"You love me?" Alabama couldn't wrap her mind around what he was saying.

Abe smiled. He'd say it over and over again until she got it. "Yes, sweet. I love you."

Alabama felt like she'd lost all her brain cells. The orgasm she'd just experienced must've sucked them all out of her head, because she'd never have said what she did next if she'd been thinking properly. "I've never been loved before."

Abe groaned and eased down beside her. He shifted so he was lying on his back and Alabama was cuddled up against his side. He slipped out of her and they both moaned at the loss. "I love you, Alabama Ford Smith.

You might never have been loved before, but you are now. Get used to it."

"Bossy," Alabama murmured, half asleep. She'd never felt this good, this safe, this protected, this...loved in all her life.

Abe squeezed her. This is where she was meant to be. In his arms.

Just before he slipped off to sleep he heard her murmur softly, "I love you, too."

He smiled, and slept better than he had in weeks.

Chapter Eleven

ALABAMA SMILED AS she cleaned. It'd been three weeks since Christopher had told her he loved her and Alabama could still hardly believe it. Her life had changed so much in the short time she'd been dating Christopher. She'd come out of her shell more and more, and she actually enjoyed spending time with his teammates.

Of course it seemed like each time they'd gone out, Faulkner, Kason, Hunter, and Sam had a new girlfriend, but she'd loved getting to know Caroline. She was funny and so smart. Alabama felt awkward around her at first. Caroline was a freakin' chemist, for God's sake, and Alabama was merely a janitor, but Caroline never made her feel less because of it.

Alabama hadn't wanted to tell Christopher what she did for a living, but it seemed absurd not to. She'd stressed about it for a week before finally just blurting it out after they'd made love one night. He'd only laughed and asked her how long she'd been trying to gain the courage to tell him. She'd blushed. He knew her too well.

All he'd said was, "I love you, sweet. I don't care what you do, just that you enjoy it. I bet you're the best damn janitor the Wolfe's have ever had." She'd laughed and admitted that Greg and Stacy Wolfe had begged her to stay with them after the fire. They'd even paid her for a week's worth of work when there'd been nothing to clean.

Caroline had been the same way. She'd not even cared what Alabama did for a living. She brushed over it like it wasn't a big deal and proceeded to ask what she thought of Hunter's new girlfriend. After he'd dumped Michele, he'd seemed even more restless than before. Not one to gossip, Alabama had just shrugged and listened as Caroline proceeded to tell her all the gossip about the guys on the team.

Alabama hadn't seen Adelaide much after their run-in in the offices a few weeks ago. It wasn't unusual, after all Alabama did clean after regular work hours were over, but she did run into some of the other agents and they were pleasant. Overall the job wasn't hard. It wasn't what Alabama wanted to do for the rest of her life, but for now it suited her. And Christopher was right. She was good at it. She took pride in her work and made sure the offices were spotless each evening before she'd left.

Alabama left the offices with a spring in her step. Her nights were better now that she had Christopher in her life. She thanked her lucky stars every day she'd found him.

Christopher made her life easier in many ways. He'd changed the locks on her door and made sure she felt safe when he couldn't be there. He was always bringing her flowers and other small gifts. When she'd protested, he just kissed her until she stopped complaining.

Alabama took care of him in return too. She'd become more comfortable on base and he'd gotten her a guest pass. She was able to come and go as she wanted and she took advantage of that by stocking up his refrigerator with his favorite foods and drinks when he was out.

The night he'd asked her to hold out her hand and he'd placed a key in it, was one of the most amazing in her life. Christopher explained it was a key to his place and that he wanted Alabama to feel as comfortable coming and going there as she did in her own place. It meant a lot to her. She'd promptly made him a copy of the key to her place as well. Alabama had no idea Abe already had one since he'd changed the locks, and he wasn't going to tell her.

Abe loved the little things Alabama did for him. He didn't think Alabama even realized how much they meant to him. He'd tried to tell her once, but she'd blushed so hard and had gotten so flustered, Abe just let it go.

One day he'd come out of his office at the base to see his car had been detailed. She'd taken his spare set of keys and spent the morning cleaning it from top to bottom for him. When he went to Alabama's apartment from work, most of the time she'd have something made for them to eat. She hadn't lied when he'd first met her when she'd said she didn't really know how to cook, but that made the simple meals she'd made for him all the more special.

Alabama did countless other things that the other women he'd dated hadn't bothered to do as well. Abe hadn't missed them at the time, but he noticed everything Alabama did for him. She picked up his dry cleaning, she'd learned how to polish his boots for him, once she'd even borrowed Caroline's bike and rode behind him while he ran one morning. She'd been sore as hell for the next couple of days and they'd had to get creative in the bedroom, but it'd been worth it. She'd told him she just wanted to be with him and if that meant she had to exercise with him, so be it.

Abe made it clear Alabama was his, but she'd turned around and made sure Abe knew he was hers as well. He loved it. He loved her.

Abe was waiting in her apartment when she'd gotten home from work. He'd made her a big dinner, complete with steak and mashed potatoes. She'd once told him that she had no idea how to grill steak or cook meat and that she never bought it anyway because of the price.

Alabama was thrilled to see Christopher when she got home. They tried to get together each night, but sometimes it wasn't possible with his work schedule.

She went right up to him as he stood in front of her stove and put her arms around him. "Hi. Did you have a good day?"

Abe was so proud of the way she'd opened up. Very rarely did she look around the room for her evil mother before she'd speak. With him, in their homes, she never hesitated and talked all the time. Abe loved he could give Alabama that feeling of safety.

"Yeah, sweet. You? Have a good night?"

"Yeah. The offices were all empty. No issues."

"Good, I made steak for us tonight. Have a seat and I'll dish it up."

"You spoil me, Christopher."

"Good, it's about time someone did."

God, Alabama loved this man.

They ate dinner making small talk. When Alabama took the dishes to the sink to wash them, Christopher took her hand. "Those can wait; I need to talk to you."

Alabama immediately tensed. That didn't sound good. No wonder men hated it when women would tell them, "We have to talk."

"It's not as bad as I'm sure you're thinking. Come on, come sit with me."

Abe led her to the couch and sat down in his usual corner, pulling her into his arms at the same time.

"I want you to meet my family."

Alabama flinched. Whoa, that hadn't been close to what she'd thought he was going to say. "Your family?"

"Yeah, my mom and my sisters. I've told them all about you and they're dying to meet you and get to know you. I want you to meet them, too. You didn't have a good mom, and I'm sorrier than you'll ever know about that. So, I want to share mine with you."

At his words, Alabama immediately started tearing up. As far as romantic words went, it wasn't much, but they meant the world to her. He knew what she'd gone through growing up and in his own way, Christopher wanted to try to make up for it.

"What if they don't like me?" Alabama couldn't help but ask.

"Oh, sweet. They'll love you. You're the best thing that's ever happened to me. They'll see that and love you because of it."

Alabama laid her head on Christopher's chest and curled into him, tucking her hands against her cheek. She could feel his arm tighten around her. He didn't pressure her; just let her work through his request on her own.

She did want to meet them. She'd heard so much about his sisters, Susie and Alicia, and of course his mom. She'd never had a family and would do almost anything to be a part of one.

"Okay."

"Okay?"

"Yeah, okay."

Abe smiled and squeezed Alabama harder. "I'm proud of you sweet. You've made me so happy. I hope you know that."

When she didn't answer, he just smiled. "I'll call them and see what I can set up."

Alabama nodded.

"Come on. Time for bed. I need you."

Alabama sat up quickly and pulled out of his arms and headed for the bed. She needed him too. She ignored his chuckle and pulled off her shirt on the way to the bed. That stopped his laughing quickly. She giggled as he scooped her up and dropped her on her back on the bed.

Her fears of meeting his family were forgotten as Christopher showed her just how much he loved her.

Chapter Twelve

A BE WATCHED ALABAMA try to control the shaking of her hands as they walked up to his mom's little house. Abe had helped his mother buy the house after he'd been in the Navy for a while. She hadn't been able to afford anything very big when he and his sisters were growing up, and Christopher wanted to make sure she was comfortable. He wanted to return the love she'd shown to him and his sisters their entire lives.

Abe didn't ring the doorbell, but instead simply opened the door and walked in. Alabama trailed behind him, nervously clutching the bouquet of flowers she'd insisted on stopping to get before they'd arrived.

She heard feminine voices as they made their way into the house.

"Mom? We're here!" Abe called out, not stopping.

Alabama couldn't help but think back to her own childhood. If she *ever* had yelled out anything like that she'd have gotten beaten. She shuddered and tried to bring herself back to the present.

Two women came rushing from the back of the house toward them. One was short but slender. She had brown hair that swung freely around her shoulders. She was wearing a pair of shorts and a henley T-shirt. She wore tennis shoes on her feet. The other woman was a bit taller and was wearing jeans and a light sweater. She had a short pixie haircut that was extremely flattering.

The shorter woman leaped at Abe and he caught her up and swung her around.

"It's so good to see you!"

"You too squirt!"

Abe put her down and turned to greet the other woman. "Hey Leesh, it's great to see you too!"

The taller woman hugged Abe hard and said, "You too bro."

"It's about time you got here!" They heard from behind them. Everyone turned to see Christopher's mom. Alabama thought she looked exactly like what a "mom" should look like. She was average height and was carrying more weight than was socially acceptable. She looked healthy and happy.

"Mom!" Abe took a step and folded his mother into his arms. He kissed her on the cheek and pulled back, still holding her. "You look great, as usual."

"Oh, you. Introduce us to your woman." She didn't waste time on pleasantries. It was obvious she'd been waiting on them.

Abe stepped away from his mom and turned toward Alabama who'd been waiting a few steps away. He reached out, grabbed her free hand and pulled her toward them.

Alabama stumbled, not expecting his move, but Abe steadied her and brought her against his side.

"Mom, Suse, Leesh, this is Alabama."

"We're so glad to finally meet you!" Susie, the shorter woman exclaimed.

"Yeah, it's about time Chris brought you out from the rock he's been hiding you under." Alicia joked smiling.

Alabama smiled back shyly. Both his sisters were funny. She loved the ease in which they joked with Christopher.

Mrs. Powers came forward and held out her hands to Alabama.

Alabama looked up at Christopher who nodded encouragedly to her. She turned toward Bev Powers and held out her free hand.

Christopher's mom grasped her hand with both of hers and squeezed. "You have *no* idea how happy I am to meet you, Alabama."

Alabama blushed, not knowing what to say. She couldn't help but look around before answering. She was uncomfortable enough to fall back into her old habits. "Thanks, Mrs. Powers. I'm happy to meet you too."

"It's Bev. You call me Bev."

"Okay. Bev."

She beamed.

Alabama didn't know what to do. She felt awkward and Christopher's mom was still holding her hand. Christopher came to her rescue, as usual, taking the flowers she'd still been clutching in her other hand and holding them out to his mom.

"We brought these for you, Mom."

Finally letting go of Alabama's hand, Bev took the flowers. "They're beautiful. Thank you. Now, let's not stand out here in the hall. Let's go sit down so we can get to know each other better."

Abe claimed Alabama's hand and held on tight as he let his sisters and mom precede them so he could have a bit of privacy before joining them.

"You doing okay so far, sweet?"

Alabama looked up at him and answered, "Surprisingly yes. I'm still nervous, but they're really nice. You're very lucky, Christopher."

Abe smiled back. He knew she'd learn to love his family as much as he did. She was tender hearted and he knew all it'd take was a bit of friendliness and she'd open up.

They headed into the living room to join his sisters and his mom.

ALABAMA SAT ON the couch next to Susie and laughed as she pointed to pictures of Christopher when he was young. They were pouring through the photo album his mom had unearthed after dinner.

His sisters were hysterical. They had no problem laughing at themselves, as well as each other. They'd shown her naked pictures of both themselves and Christopher, but obviously took great pleasure in showing off embarrassing moments of their brother's childhood.

The stories they'd shared all night were also precious to Alabama. She had no such memories of her life, and she loved that Christopher had them.

"Hey, Chris, remember that time you came home to visit when I had a date and you actually threatened him?" Alicia recalled.

"Hey, I didn't threaten him!" Abe returned laughing. "All I did was tell him if he didn't get you home safe and sound by curfew, he'd regret it."

"Yeah, and you were sitting on the porch cleaning your gun when we got home. He didn't even kiss me good-night. He actually shook my hand. *Shook my hand!* God, it was so humiliating!"

Everyone laughed. Alabama could just imagine it. Christopher had obviously learned to be protective at a young age, but she loved it. She'd never had anything like that in her life and she would've done anything to have experienced it just once growing up. Before she thought about what she was saying she blurted out, "You guys were so lucky to have a protective older brother."

"Oh, they didn't think so at the time," Bev said laughing, "but you're right, Alabama. We're all very lucky. I don't know how I managed it, but Chris turned out all right."

Alabama could feel Christopher's eyes on her. She raised her head and saw the intense way he was looking at her. He *knew* what she was thinking. He *knew* how she grew up and how she would've done anything to have had a brother like him.

"Mom, Suse, Leesh, we're gonna have to get home." He'd said it without looking away from Alabama.

She blushed. She was embarrassed, but she was ready. The night had been stressful. Nice, but stressful. Alabama was ready to go. She wanted to come back though.

They all stood up and Alabama watched as Christopher hugged each of "his girls," then came back to her side.

"It was great meeting you, Alabama. I hope you'll come back soon. We're thrilled you're lowering yourself to date our brother." Alicia said, laughing once again.

Bev also put her two cents in. "Yes, please, come back soon. I was going to try to talk to you alone at some point tonight, but I see that Chris doesn't want to leave your side. I hope you know how much my son likes you. He's only brought one other woman home to meet us, and she wasn't nice."

Alabama blinked. Huh?

"You're nice. We like you. He wouldn't have risked bringing you here if you were only a passing fancy for him. I'm looking forward to many more dinners and lunches and get-togethers. If my son knows what's good for him, he'll put a ring on your finger sooner rather than later."

"Mom!" Abe admonished. Jesus. Now *he* was embarrassed.

"What?" Bev said not-so-innocently. "I just wanted to make sure Alabama knew this wasn't an everyday occurrence for you."

"Jeez, Mom, do you think I haven't already told her that?"

Alabama tried to smother a laugh. For once it was nice to see Christopher embarrassed instead of her. She squeezed his hand. "It's okay, Christopher." She tried to soothe him.

Everyone laughed, breaking the tension.

"Okay, we're leaving. I'll call you guys as soon as I can. Stay safe."

Everyone got hugs, including Alabama, which was a bit awkward for her, but she returned the embraces as if they were her due.

Abe settled Alabama into the passenger seat of his car then walked around and climbed into the driver's seat. Before starting the car, he turned toward Alabama and wrapped his hand around the back of her neck and pulled her toward him. He rested his forehead against hers and whispered, "Thank you, sweet."

Alabama grasped his wrist with her hands and said, "For what?"

"Thank you for coming with me today. It means more to me than I can say that you like my family."

"They're good people, Christopher. I'm just glad they didn't hate me."

"There's no chance they would've hated you, baby. They loved you. They would've moved you into my place today if you'd given them half a chance."

She laughed. "I'm not sure about that, but I loved seeing you guys together. You have no idea how lucky you are."

"I know, Alabama. Believe me, I know. I spend too much time in crappy countries and see way too many examples of horrible things people do to one another to take advantage of my family…or you."

Alabama caressed the back of his neck with one of her hands. "I know you do, Christopher. You deserve your family."

"You deserve my family too, sweet."

They sat in the car for another moment before Abe closed his eyes and touched his lips to hers. The kiss was light and sweet, but wasn't short.

They pulled back and sat for a few seconds looking into each other's eyes.

"You ready to head home?" Abe asked with an intense look in his eyes.

Alabama knew exactly what was on his mind, and it was on hers too. She nodded.

Abe kissed her one more time, then let go and turned the key in the ignition. "Let's go home, sweet. I'll show you how much I 'like' you." He smirked.

Alabama couldn't wait.

Chapter Thirteen

T HE NEXT NIGHT after cleaning the offices, Alabama entered Christopher's quarters on the base. He'd told her to come to his place because he wanted to make her dinner. She much preferred it when he made dinner because she sucked at it. She could make packaged noodles or stew, but that was about the extent of her culinary skills.

The moment she opened his door she smelled the delicious scent of garlic and other spices. He was making spaghetti and it smelled heavenly.

Abe couldn't wait for Alabama to get off work and get home. He'd started thinking about anyplace they were sleeping each night as "home." He wanted to spoil her tonight because he'd gotten the news he'd been dreading for a while. He knew it was going to come sooner or later, and today their commanding officer told them they were slated for a mission.

They were leaving the next morning, which wasn't surprising. Most of the time when they got called away, it was with little-to-no notice.

Now Abe had to tell Alabama he was leaving. He was nervous. It was the first time the team had been called away on a mission since he and Alabama had gotten together.

Abe wasn't stupid. He knew the statistics of relationships of Navy SEALS. They were abysmally low. But if Caroline and Wolf would make it work, Abe had hope that he and Alabama could as well.

This first time he had to leave Alabama would be tough, he knew it. For the first time in a long time, Abe wasn't looking forward to leaving. Usually he was the first person on the plane and was the most enthusiastic about completing the mission successfully.

This would be the first time Abe didn't spend the night before they left going over the intelligence they'd received. He wanted to spend every second with Alabama, not thinking about work. Abe wanted to answer any questions Alabama had, that he was allowed to answer, and he wanted to spend his last hours with her wrapped in his arms.

"Hey, sweet, did you have a good day?" Abe went to meet Alabama as she came into the room.

"Yeah, same ol', same ol'. You?"

"I missed you."

"Well, duh," Alabama returned with a smirk.

Abe laughed and grabbed her. He bent her over his

arm and leaned her backwards until her head was below her shoulders.

Alabama shrieked and grabbed his biceps tightly. Abe put his mouth on her neck and nipped. "You missed me?" He asked between bites.

"Yes, yes, you know I did! Let me up!"

Abe chuckled and brought her upright, not letting go.

Alabama could feel how happy he was to see her. His hard length pressed against her as he held her close.

"Kiss me, sweet. It's been almost eight hours since I've tasted you."

"With pleasure."

After a few moments Abe reluctantly pulled away. "If I don't stop now, we don't get to eat."

"That's okay with me," Alabama murmured before pulling his earlobe into her mouth and sucking, hard.

Abe shuddered and thought about saying the hell with dinner before remembering he had to tell her he was leaving in the morning.

He set Alabama away firmly and laughed as she pouted. "Come on, let me feed you, woman."

Dinner was delicious, as usual. Christopher was a wonderful cook and Alabama always enjoyed whatever he made. The sauce for the noodles was spicy, but not overwhelmingly so.

When they'd finished, they both cleared the table

and Christopher washed the dishes while Alabama dried them.

"Want to watch television for a while?" Abe asked, knowing she'd decline.

"No, I want you."

Alabama had come out of her shell and Abe loved it. She didn't seem shy with him anymore and she was confident in bed. He loved that she let him be as bossy as he needed to be. She'd do whatever he told her to with no questions asked. He'd told her one night that if there was ever anything he asked of her in the bedroom that she didn't feel comfortable doing, she should tell him and he'd back off. Abe had been surprised by her response. Alabama told him that she trusted him. That she loved when he took charge and she'd loved everything they'd done together. Abe knew they were meant to be together.

Abe grabbed Alabama and slung her over his shoulder in a fireman's hold. At her surprised shriek, he laughed.

"Put me down, Christopher, I'm too heavy!"

"Are you kidding me? Baby, you know I'm a SEAL right? The equipment I have to carry weighs more than you do!"

She laughed with him. He stopped laughing when he felt her hands gripping his butt. He walked faster toward his bed. He had to be inside her. Now.

He stalked into his bedroom and dumped Alabama in the middle of his bed. Abe loved the sound of her laughter, loved being the one to give that to her. He knew she hadn't laughed enough in her life.

"I love seeing you here."

"Where?"

"In my bed."

Alabama smiled up at Christopher and sat up. Without a word she lifted both arms above her head.

Abe reached for Alabama and slowly tugged her shirt over her head. Without looking to see where it landed, he threw it behind him. He reached for her breasts and caressed them. "God, Alabama, you are so fucking sexy."

Alabama just smiled up at Christopher. She could see the evidence of how sexy he thought she looked, by the hard ridge in his pants. She laid back, dislodging his hands. Resting on her elbows on the bed, she told him playfully, "These pants are awfully uncomfortable. Care to help me with them?"

Abe loved when Alabama got playful. "Of course, sweet. Wouldn't want you to be uncomfortable..." Running his hands over her stomach he took his time in getting to the button on her jeans. He released it and slowly eased the zipper down. "Lift up," he ordered hoarsely and swallowed hard when Alabama lifted her hips up at him.

Abe put his hands inside her jeans at either side of

her hips and eased the material down, taking her undies with them at the same time. "Whoops, looks like your panties accidentally came off with your jeans."

Alabama just laughed and reached behind her back and unclipped her bra. She quickly removed it and laid back, hands over her head, and arched her back. "One of us is overdressed."

Without a word Abe pulled Alabama's hips to the side of the bed. She shrieked in surprise, but he didn't hesitate. He looked up and caught her eyes with his and lowered his head.

"Christopher," Alabama moaned in ecstasy.

Finally taking his eyes from hers, Abe looked down at the perfection that was Alabama's sex. "You're so wet." He took one hand from her hips and ran his finger lightly through her wetness and up to her clit, then he lowered his head. While his finger caressed over and around her hot spot, his tongue explored every inch of her folds.

Alabama moaned. She never dreamed oral sex could feel this good. She and Christopher had played and explored each other's bodies, but this was different somehow. He was still completely dressed and she loved it. She felt wanton and sexy and she loved every second of his mouth on her. "God, that feels so good."

Abe moved his mouth up to her clit, and lightly sucked. He eased his finger inside her at the same time and searched for the soft spot on the front wall of her sex. When Alabama jumped in his grasp, he knew he'd found it. He eased another finger inside to join the first while his other hand gripped her hip tightly. Abe lifted his head long enough to murmur, "Let go, sweet. I want to feel you come around my fingers. Give me all you got, don't hold back." He lowered his head and set about driving her crazy.

Alabama writhed in Christopher's grasp. She put one hand on the back of his head and gripped what little hair he had. Her other hand gripped the sheet at her side tightly. She'd orgasmed with Christopher inside her before, but this was different somehow. It seemed more intimate, more intense…just more.

Abe could feel Alabama was close. He stroked her inner wall and sucked hard on her clit at the same time. With one last twist of his hand and a little hum under his breath, Alabama was coming for him.

He didn't let up as she thrashed under him, but kept going until she shuddered again. Finally when she moaned, "God, please, Christopher," he eased up. He licked her one more time and slowly removed his fingers. Waiting until she looked down at him, he brought his fingers to his mouth and slowly cleaned off her juices. "Beautiful and delicious," he told her with a gleam in his eye.

"I want you."

"You have me, sweet."

"No, inside. I want you inside me. Now."

Abe slowly backed away from the side of the bed where he'd been kneeling and stood up. "Scoot back, sweet. Give me some room."

Alabama did as he asked, and moved to the center of the bed, not taking her eyes off of Christopher. As she moved, he whipped his shirt up and over his head, then removed his pants and underwear without taking his eyes off of her. Within moments he was moving over her on the bed.

She looked up at his as he came over her. His eyes were intense and dilated with lust. Without a word he finally broke eye contact and leaned down and captured one breast in his hand and the other with his mouth. He alternated sucking and pinching her nipples. Finally when Alabama was ready to attack him, he said, "I can't wait anymore."

"Then don't. Jesus, Christopher. Take me already."

"Guide me in."

Alabama moaned. Everything out of his mouth was sexy as hell and turned her on even more. She reached down and caressed Christopher's impressive hard on. When he growled at her, she just smiled.

"Do it."

Alabama would've teased him further, but she wanted him inside her as much as he apparently wanted to be there. She guided his length to her opening and they moved at the same time. She thrust her hips up just as he pushed into her with one quick movement.

"Oh yeah," he moaned at the same time Alabama said, "God, yes!"

Abe held himself still over Alabama for a moment. She felt amazing. Every time they made love felt like the first time all over again. She gripped him tight and she was soaking wet. He pulled out to the tip, then thrust in to the hilt. He wanted to lose himself in her, to somehow make them one. He pulled out again, slowly, then slammed inside once more.

"Yeah, Christopher. Again. Harder."

Abe did as Alabama asked, and repeated his movement. Over and over, he slowly pulled out, then slammed back inside her. When her hips started thrusting up to meet his on each down stroke, he flipped them. Alabama faltered at the change in position and leaned up to look down at him. Her hands rested on his chest and he could feel them flex into little claws.

"Ride me, Alabama. Take me."

Without a word she moved. She pulled herself up, then back down. It look her a few strokes to get into a rhythm, but once she did, they both groaned.

"You are beautiful. Look at you." Abe couldn't believe how lucky he was. Alabama *was* beautiful. Her breasts bounced with her movements and her head was thrown back. He ran his hands down over her chest and gripped her hips tightly in his. "Harder, Alabama. I'm yours. Take me."

When Abe knew he was on the verge, he reached down and ran his thumb over Alabama's clit as she rode him. Three strokes was all it took before she exploded. He took over and held her hips tight as she shook above him and slammed himself into her. After five strokes, he too was coming. Abe held Alabama to him as they rode out their orgasms. Finally Alabama collapsed on top of him.

"I'm too heavy," Alabama murmured and tried to slide off to the side of his body.

"No, you're perfect. Stay. I don't want to lose you yet." That too was a new experience for Abe. In the past he couldn't wait to retreat from a woman's bed and clean himself up. He couldn't take a shower soon enough after he left the bed. But with Alabama, he reveled in their combined scent, her touch, the feel of himself softening inside of her. He was going to miss this. He was going to miss her. Fuck, he didn't want to leave her.

They lay in bed entwined and sated. Every time they'd made love it seemed to get better and better. Alabama had finally slid to the side and her head was now resting on his shoulder and she had one leg thrown over his. Her arm was tight around his abdomen and she was snuggled into his side as if she was attached.

Abe knew it was time. He couldn't put off the news of his leaving any longer. He hated to do it when they were both so relaxed, but it had to be done.

"Sweet, our commanding officer called the team in today with news. I have to leave tomorrow on a mission. I can't tell you where we're going or how long we'll be gone, but I swear to you, I'll be back as soon as I can."

Tears immediately sprung to Alabama's eyes. She knew this day was coming. They'd been lucky so far, the team hadn't been called out in a long time. She didn't let go of Christopher, but tilted her head back so she could see his face.

"Don't cry sweet, I'll be back soon," Abe begged.

"That's not why I'm upset," Alabama choked out.

"Talk to me."

"You'll be careful, won't you?"

"Oh, baby." Abe knew immediately what she was scared of. "Of course. You know my team is the best of the best. Besides, I have *you* to come back home to. I won't be taking any chances. I want to come home to you."

"Promise?"

Abe smiled. She'd made him promise all sorts of things since they'd been dating, and he hadn't hesitated to promise whatever she needed to hear. He'd lasso the moon if he could for her.

"I promise, sweet."

She sniffed loudly and tried to bring herself under control. "Maybe I'll call Caroline and hang out with her while you guys are gone."

Abe tilted her chin up and kissed her passionately. He loved how sensitive Alabama was. She went from being upset he'd be gone, to immediately thinking about her friend and how she'd need some support as well.

"That's a great idea. I know she'd love to have some company while we're gone. You know you could also call Susie or Alicia too. I'm sure they'd love to get to know you better."

Alabama nodded and cuddled deeper into Christopher's arms. She wasn't ready to meet with his sisters by herself. She knew it'd take a few more visits with Christopher with her before she'd be ready to go out with them on her own.

They were silent for a while, lost in their own thoughts. Finally, Abe turned Alabama until she was on her back and he loomed over her. He smiled. Yeah, he didn't want to leave, but the sooner he left, the sooner he could get back and have out-of-this-world "welcome home" sex. In the meantime he meant to leave his woman so satiated they'd be able to make it through their separation.

Chapter Fourteen

A LABAMA SAT AT her small kitchen table twirling a fork around her fingers while she waited for her microwave dinner to finish. It'd been ten days since Christopher had left and she felt bereft. She and Caroline had gotten together several nights and talked. Alabama got a better idea what it meant to be with a SEAL. Many times the SEAL team had to leave at a moment's notice. Caroline never knew where Matthew was or when he'd be back.

But Caroline had explained while it was tough, very tough, she also knew it was what Matthew was meant to do. Because of her experiences with the team, she knew they were competent at what they did. Caroline had told Alabama the entire story about how she'd been kidnapped and thrown overboard in the ocean. The SEAL team had come together and not only saved her life, but brought down the bad guys at the same time.

Alabama had been horrified at what Caroline had been through, but understood what Caroline was trying to tell her. Caroline trusted the team to take care of each other—she'd seen them first hand in action.

Caroline loved the other men on the team like brothers. There was no one she'd rather have at Matthew's back then the men on the team. Alabama figured if Caroline could trust them to keep Matthew safe, then she could do the same with Christopher.

Alabama came back to the present. Work that night had been weird. She'd shown up as usual at the Realty building, but Adelaide had been there with another agent, Joni. Alabama didn't really know Joni that well. She'd joined the company after the fire. Alabama had seen Adelaide and Joni hanging out, so she hadn't bothered to try to get to know her. She figured if Joni was hanging out with Adelaide, she had no desire to *get* to know her. Maybe that wasn't fair, but it was what it was.

Alabama had gone to get her cart ready for the night's cleaning when Joni had come up behind her. She'd scared the crap out of Alabama, but she tried to brush it off.

"Hey, Alabama. How're you tonight?"

Alabama was surprised Joni was talking to her, even more surprised than she'd been at seeing them in the office after hours.

"I'm good. How are you?" She'd gotten so much better at small talk since she'd started dating Christopher and hanging out with his team.

"Good. So, how long do you usually work each night? It has to suck working nights huh?"

"It's not so bad. I'm usually done in a couple of hours."

"Ah, yeah, that's not too bad. Okay, well, I'm out of here. Have a good night."

Alabama watched warily as Joni walked back down the hall. Not too much later she saw Adelaide and Joni leaving together. She shrugged and continued with her work. She couldn't care too much about them. She'd learned what really mattered in life. Christopher. He was out working to protect their country; she couldn't worry about catty women like Adelaide.

ALABAMA CHANGED INTO her flannel pajamas and snuggled down into her bed. She'd had to do laundry yesterday and she felt so hollow lying in her bed now. While the sheets smelled fresh and clean, she missed smelling Christopher. His scent had permeated the pillowcases and sheets, but tonight she couldn't smell him.

It wasn't only the lack of his scent that made her melancholy. They'd done so many wonderful things in her bed. Alabama had gotten used to sleeping with Christopher; she'd had a hard time adjusting to sleeping alone again.

Alabama jerked awake when she heard a key in her lock. She sat up straight in bed and watched as the door opened. She shrieked a girly shriek, seeing it was Christopher. He was home!

Abe braced himself as Alabama leaped across the small room and threw herself at him. He grunted as she made contact with his body and went back on a foot. He dropped his duffel bag and gathered her close. God he'd missed her. She smelled so good. He was tired. When they'd gotten back to the base, he'd thought about going back to his place to get some much needed sleep and coming over to her apartment in the morning, but he couldn't make himself do it. He hadn't even taken a shower before coming to her apartment.

He needed to see her. He needed to feel her in his arms. The mission hadn't been terribly difficult, but it seemed twice as long this time. Now that he had Alabama waiting for him back at home, the mission seemed harder. He'd talked to Wolf about it and they'd had some good discussions about what it meant to have someone at home. Wolf had gone through the same thing.

Every single thing they did while fighting for their country had a deeper meaning now that they had someone waiting for them. It wasn't that they were careless before, but now, every single decision they made could mean their woman would never see them again. It was tough. Wolf helped Abe try to work through it in his mind.

Alabama didn't hesitate to wrap her arms and legs around Christopher. Thank God he was home. She buried her nose in his neck…then drew back. Whoa. He stunk. He certainly didn't smell like the man she knew and loved. She watched as Christopher grinned.

"I gotta shower, sweet."

"Yeah, I can see and smell that."

"I had to see you. I didn't want to wait."

Okay, that was sweet. She smiled, dropping her legs and standing, but not letting go of him. "I'm glad you didn't. I love you."

"Jesus. I love you too." Abe gathered her close again and they stood there for a bit enjoying the feel of being back in each other's arms.

"Okay, to the shower with you. Do you have clothes that need to be put in the wash? Do you want something to eat or drink?"

"No sweet. Thank you. It can wait until morning. All I want is to get clean then get in you." He watched as she blushed. He loved she could still blush at his frank talk. "Go crawl in bed and get naked, I'll be there in a second."

Alabama nodded and backed away from him. She'd never get used to his dirty talk, but secretly she loved it.

She brought her hands up to the buttons on her shirt and started unbuttoning them from the bottom. "Hurry up, Christopher. I'll be waiting."

She laughed as he stumbled on his way to the small bathroom in her apartment. She loved being able to surprise him. It didn't happen very often so when it did, it was awesome.

Abe took the quickest shower he could and still get the stink and grime off of him. The bandage on his shoulder had to come off, since it had gotten wet, but he didn't think he needed another after he was done. He whisked the towel over his body and quickly shaved the stubble off his chin. As much as he enjoyed the thought of leaving his mark on Alabama, he didn't want to hurt her. He strode out of the bathroom with the towel draped around his waist and stopped dead in his tracks at the sight of Alabama in the bed.

She was completely naked and lying on top of the covers. She'd propped herself against the pillows and was reclining against the headboard. Her knees were bent and her legs were open. She was running her hands over her chest, up and down and occasionally running her fingers down her inner thigh. "It's about time."

Abe strode quickly to the bed, losing the towel on the way. It fell forlornly onto the ground, immediately forgotten. "Hell, you are amazing."

Alabama was all ready to seduce her boyfriend. She

felt awkward as hell touching herself, but if his reaction was anything to go by, it was worth it. Just as he got to the bed and put a knee on the mattress to crawl over to her, she saw the wound on his shoulder.

Alabama gasped and immediately closed her legs and stopped touching herself. "Oh my God! Christopher, you're hurt!"

"No, sweet, it's nothing. Now come here."

"No! You're hurt. Let me see."

Abe sighed. He really needed her, but it didn't look like she was going to cooperate, at least not yet. He could've ordered her to get back in place, but he didn't have it in him at the moment. It'd actually feel good to have her fuss over him.

Alabama leaned over and turned the light on next to the bed. She seemed to have no idea how sexy she was fussing over him totally nude. Abe tried to ignore how her body swayed and jiggled in all the right places, but it was no use. He'd spent the last week and a half in a hell hole on the other side of the world missing her. He wasn't going to be able to wait to be inside her for long.

Alabama inspected Christopher's shoulder. He was right, it wasn't bad, but it did look deep. "What happened?" She inquired softly, running her fingers lightly over the stitches in his shoulder.

"A bad guy with a knife got a bit closer than I'd have liked."

Ignoring all the implications of what he'd said, Alabama tried to tamp down her curiosity. Most likely she really didn't want to know what really happened. She'd probably have nightmares if she did know.

"Did you guys win?"

Abe chuckled. He'd been prepared to deflect her questions about the mission itself. He couldn't talk about it, even with her. But she'd surprised him again. He shouldn't have been though. It seemed she understood.

"Yeah, sweet, we won." It wasn't like it was a contest, but he didn't bother to explain that to her. He figured she knew that though, her words just came out wrong.

Abe clenched his teeth as Alabama leaned toward him and kissed the ten stitches in his shoulder. He'd killed the man even as the knife was glancing off his shoulder. It'd gotten him where the Kevlar vest hadn't quite covered him. It was a lucky strike, too bad it wasn't lucky enough. The man was dead before he'd hit the ground.

The feel of Alabama's tongue on his skin was the last straw. Abe flipped her over and pinned her under him. She smiled up at him.

"I missed you, Christopher," she said sweetly. "I'm glad you're home."

"Me too, sweet. Me too."

They spent the next few hours showing each other how much they'd missed each other. The sun had just started to peek over the horizon when they finally fell into exhausted slumber, both secure in the fact the other was close and safe.

Chapter Fifteen

ALABAMA SAT IN the hard chair shaking. The tabletop in front of her was a shiny stainless steel, without even a single fingerprint on it. She wondered how they got it so clean. Vaguely, she also wondered what kind of cleaner they used on it. She tried not to think about how long it'd been since she'd been told Christopher had been called. The police officer hadn't let her call him herself, but said he'd pass the word along she was here and she wanted to see him. He'd come soon, Alabama just had to keep telling herself that.

She was freezing. They must keep the temperature unnaturally cool so people would confess or something. She had no idea, she only knew she was cold and couldn't wait for Christopher to come and help her make sense out of what was going on. He'd told her again and again he'd look after her. She definitely needed him to "look after her" now.

That morning was one of the best of her life. She'd woken up in Christopher's arms much later than usual after their late night of passion. He'd sleepily kissed her and told her he loved her. He'd been exhausted. She supposed missions would do that, not to mention their late night antics in bed.

She'd gotten up and made him brunch. He hadn't had to go in early because of their late night return, but he'd told her he had to go in to debrief that afternoon. They'd made plans to get together later after her shift at work.

When she'd arrived at Wolfe Realty, it was to find the place in an uproar. She wasn't sure exactly what had happened, but the next thing she knew, she was in handcuffs and being brought to the police station.

Alabama was terrified. Nothing like this had ever happened to her before. Her experience with police officers wasn't the best, and she was scared. She'd begged to be able to call Christopher, and they hadn't let her. Finally, seeing she was losing it, she was told they'd call and explain things to him. She didn't like that, but she supposed it was the best deal she'd get at the moment.

Alabama knew something wasn't right when the officer who'd said he'd call Christopher re-entered the room without him.

"Is he coming?" Alabama asked nervously. He'd come. He'd be there. He promised to take care of her.

"Uh, he's on his way, but first he's answering some

questions."

"You can't do that!" Alabama immediately exclaimed. "He doesn't have anything to do with this. Leave him alone! He's a hero to his country, he just got back from a mission. You can't do that!"

The officer was obviously taken aback by her outburst. She knew he hadn't expected her quick and passionate defense of Christopher.

"Calm down, lady. He was the one who wanted to have some words with my boss before he came in to talk to you."

His words did calm Alabama down. Okay, she got it. Christopher was trying to figure out the best way to get her out of this. He'd know this was all bullcrap and he'd get her out of here. They'd be laughing about it later tonight.

When the door opened a second time Alabama looked up and sighed in relief. Finally.

Alabama watched as Christopher opened the door and kept one hand on the knob and stood by the door. She nervously stood up. She looked at him and tensed. He was pissed. She didn't know at who or why, but it was obvious he was holding his anger in check by his fingernails.

Alabama took one step towards him. "Christopher?"

He looked away from her and at the officer still standing in the room. "Can I have a minute?"

"Sure, but you know protocol." He pointed up at the little camera in the corner of the room. Obviously they'd be taping whatever conversation she had with Christopher.

Abe nodded tightly and stepped out of the way so the officer could leave the room.

"Thank God, you're here!" Alabama exclaimed in relief and took another step in Christopher's direction. She was stunned to see him take a step sideways, away from her. She stopped in her tracks a good four feet from him. What the hell? Her heart sped up in her chest. What was going on?

"Why'd you do it, Alabama?" Abe asked tensely. "Why'd you steal that crap? You know I'd give you anything you wanted. There was no reason to take it."

Alabama stood stunned. He actually thought she'd *done* what they accused her of? She wasn't sure what to say, but it obviously didn't matter to Christopher, he was still talking.

"I *told* you how I feel about stealing. You heard how my nickname came about. We talked about it. You *knew* and you still did it. It feels like you purposely were trying to sabotage our relationship. What was last night about then? One last fuck? Can you explain why the hell you threw us away? Huh? Can you?"

"Threw us away?" Alabama asked incredulously in a shaking voice. What was he saying? She couldn't gather

her thoughts. If she thought she was scared before, now she was downright terrified. Christopher was supposed to be here helping her figure out what the hell happened. He should be holding her tight in his arms. In all the time they'd been together he'd always protected her from this sort of thing. He'd never let anyone raise their voice to her the way he was doing right now. What happened between the time when they'd last seen each other that afternoon, and now?

"Christopher, I…"

"*Shut up,* Alabama, I don't really want to hear your excuses right now."

Alabama could literally feel her heart shrivel up and die at his words. She took a step back as if he'd punched her. She felt like throwing up. He knew what his words would do to her. He *knew.* He was right, they *had* talked about it. She'd spilled her guts about her mama and the things she'd said to her. Christopher knew telling her to "shut up" was the one thing she couldn't handle. He knew it and did it anyway, shattering her in the process.

"All I ever wanted from you was an honest relationship. I was ready to give you everything I had. You could've had it all. I would've laid it all at your feet. My protection, my love, my family; but instead you *had* to have that money. I hope it was worth it."

Alabama really had nothing to say. After all they'd

been through. She'd told him she loved him. He'd claimed to love her in return, but it was obviously all a ploy to get her into bed, or something. He was so ready to listen to others and not even to hear what she had to say and it killed her. But him telling her to shut up, gutted her.

"You promised." The words came out soft and tortured. She looked him in the eyes and repeated, "You promised, Christopher."

She watched as he slightly flinched at her words. But she didn't care. She was done. She was empty inside. She'd thought she'd finally found someone who would be there for her. Who loved her as she was. Who would stand by her and help her make her way through the world and be her refuge. *Shut up, Alabama. Shut up, Alabama. Shut up, Alabama.* His words echoed through her brain over and over. Every time slicing at her as if it was the first time she'd heard them.

Alabama turned around and sat in the chair she'd so eagerly vacated at his entrance into the room. She calmly pulled the chair up to the table, clasped her hands in her lap and stared at the wall on the far side of the room blankly. Christopher's voice morphed into her mama's. *Shut up. Shut up. Shut up.* She cringed, remembering the feel of Mama's fists and feet as she hit her over and over.

Alabama couldn't think. She just had to make it

through the next five minutes. Then the next. Then the next. It was how she'd made it through those awful times Mama had locked her in the closet. It was how she'd made it through most of her life before Christopher had crashed his way into her heart. She counted her breaths. One. Two. Three. She had to keep breathing.

She vaguely heard Christopher talking, but she blocked him out. Nothing he said mattered anymore. Alabama could feel her heart beating unnaturally fast, but sat still, not saying anything.

Finally she heard the door shut. She was alone in the room. She was alone, as she should've remembered she'd always be. It was her against the world. No matter what anyone said. No matter what anyone tried to convince her otherwise. She'd forgotten for a while. She'd forgotten the lessons Mama had taught her. That the high school football player who'd humiliated her so long ago had taught her.

Abe smacked the door to the police station hard as he left the building. Damn Alabama to hell. He'd woken up this morning happier than he'd ever been in his life. The debriefing of the mission had been tough. They'd all had to rehash their actions and make sure they'd done everything right. Through the debriefing they'd discovered some things that could've gone better and Abe knew those things were *his* fault. His head wasn't one hundred percent in the game. He'd messed up.

Then he'd gotten a call from Cookie, who'd heard from his old girlfriend, Michele, that Alabama had been arrested at her job. Apparently Michele had gotten the whole sordid story from Adelaide. Alabama had been stealing money from the agents for a while now. She'd clean their offices at night and take stuff from their desks. At first it was little things, candy from candy bowls, pens, that sort of thing. Then money started going missing. Jewelry.

They'd found some of the missing items on her cleaning cart. There was a secret pocket sewn into the side of the material. She was caught red-handed.

His Alabama was a thief. His heart broke and he felt sick. How could she do this? *Why* was she doing it? Wolf had tried to talk to him, but Abe's phone rang. It was an officer at the police station calling to tell him Alabama had requested to see him.

He'd gone straight to the station without telling Wolf and his other teammates what had happened. He was too pissed, too embarrassed that his girlfriend was apparently a thief.

He'd spoken to the chief when he'd arrived at the station. He'd outlined the charges against Alabama and what evidence there was. They were doing interviews with some of the witnesses now, then they'd interrogate

Alabama.

Jesus. Interrogate her.

Abe had seen red. All of it had been a lie. What else had she lied about? Was her pitiful story about her childhood even true? Did he even *know* her? He'd stormed into the room where she was being held and confronted her.

Abe sat in the front seat of his car with his head on the steering wheel. His heart hurt. What had just happened?

He'd been so *pissed*. He'd gone into that room not knowing what he was going to say to her and every time she'd opened her mouth to try to explain, he'd cut her off. He didn't want to hear her lies.

Abe recalled the look on Alabama's face when he'd told her to "shut up." He'd seen her close down right in front of him. One minute she was there trying to talk to him, the next it was like she was gone. A veil had come over her eyes and she was just gone. She'd spoken two words to him, *you promised*, and the Alabama he'd known over the last few months was gone. He'd known she wasn't hearing him after that. She'd gone and sat back down at the table and refused to look at him. It had to be an admission of guilt; she was ignoring him because everything he'd said was right on the money.

He rubbed a hand over his eyes a few times and then back over his head. God he was tired. He hadn't caught up on the sleep he'd missed on the mission, and last night's passion filled night with Alabama hadn't helped. He couldn't think. He didn't want to think.

Abe pulled out of the parking lot and headed for the base. He'd think tomorrow. Tonight he just needed to sleep.

ALABAMA HADN'T SAID a word since Christopher left. There was no point. She had nothing. No one. The officers tried to get her to talk, but she sat stonily in front of them staring off into space. They'd showed her the evidence against her, including pictures of the hidden pocket sewn into the cleaning cart.

When they'd gotten no reaction, they'd tried to scare her into confessing. Still, she sat as still as a statue, not saying a word. Finally, they had no choice but to book her into the county jail.

As Abe was settling into a restless sleep in his room on the base, Alabama was being fingerprinted and booked. She'd had to change into a pair of county-issued orange elastic pants and scrub-type shirt. She'd been roughly led to the third floor of the county building in Riverton, and locked into a small dank room that smelled slightly of body odor. Her roommate tried to talk to her, but getting no response, shrugged and settled back on her mattress.

Alabama lay on the top bunk in the jail cell wondering how her day had gone from the best day of her life to the worst in a matter of hours. A lone tear fell down her temple before she locked it down. *Shut up. Shut up. Shut up.* She squeezed her eyes shut and tried to block out the words. She counted her breaths. One. Two Three…

Chapter Sixteen

ABE HAD HAD time to think about everything that had happened in the last few days and knew he made a mistake. *Knew* he'd made the biggest mistake in his life. Problem was, he had no idea how to fix it. He shouldn't have opened his mouth. He should've let Alabama talk to him. He'd never forget the look in her eyes when he'd told her to shut up if he lived to be a hundred. He knew what he was doing when he'd said it, and that made him even more of a bastard. Abe knew he'd marked Alabama when he saw the shield fall down over her eyes. It as if one minute she was there, and the next she wasn't.

He wasn't thinking straight when he'd left the station. It wasn't until a couple of days later that he wondered what was happening to Alabama. He thought she would've tried to call him by now. Now that he'd gotten some sleep, he'd begun to be able to think clearly again. He'd gone through the last couple of days in a haze. Cookie had called asking what was up his butt and

Abe told him the entire sordid story.

"So when I went to the police station I was pissed. Pissed at myself, pissed at my dad, pissed at her. After everything she'd been through in her life, I didn't let her explain. I cut her off and told her to shut up."

Abe heard Cookie's indrawn breath and quickly defended himself. "I heard my dad's words ringing in my ears. His excuses. I didn't mean it."

"You didn't mean it, but you said it anyway. You can't take something like that back. Once it's out there, it's out there. You know it Abe," had been Cookie's response, and he'd hung up on him. That was two days ago and Abe hadn't heard from anyone else on the team since then.

Abe now knew deep in his gut that Alabama was innocent and that Adelaide was behind whatever had happened. He didn't know how he knew it, but it had to be the reason Alabama had been arrested. Adelaide been pissed at Alabama for supposedly stealing him away from her. That hadn't been the case, but there was no reasoning with a jealous woman.

As soon as Abe realized Alabama was innocent, he'd thought in horror about what she was going through. What had happened when he left that night? Had she been arrested? Did they send her home? What if they'd arrested her? Panic started clawing through Abe. Cookie was right, he *was* a dumb ass.

Abe started trying to fix the wrong he'd done by calling Cookie. He didn't answer. He systematically tried each of his other teammates and no one answered. He even called the police department and was told Ms. Smith had bonded out. Abe wanted to throw up. Bonded out. Fuck. That means they'd arrested her. He hoped she'd been able to pay the fine that night, but when he'd inquired about when she left, he was told Alabama had spent three nights and two days locked up.

Shit. Just shit. This was his fault. He had to fix it.

You promised.

The words wouldn't leave his head. They repeated over and over. He *had* promised, and at the first sign of trouble he'd left her high and dry. Some hero he was. He felt horrible. He had to fix this.

He headed over to her apartment. He'd find her there and they'd talk. He wouldn't let her take no for an answer. He'd apologize and then set about fixing what he'd broken between them. Abe couldn't imagine another scenario. He loved her. She had to forgive him.

Abe stood inside Alabama's apartment and looked around in shock. It was empty. All her things were gone. The couch was still there. The bed too. But the little vase that had been sitting on the kitchen table and had held the many flowers he'd brought her was gone. The bright blanket that had covered her bed, gone. The movies they'd watched together that had been stacked up against the TV stand, gone.

You promised.

Abe walked over to the refrigerator and opened it. Empty. Suddenly in a flurry of motion he threw open cabinets, hoping against hope to find some sign of Alabama. There was nothing.

He sagged against the counter. Jesus. Where had she gone?

Abe startled badly when a voice came from the open door. It was the old woman who he'd winked at several times as he saw her peeking out her door as he and Alabama would pass by.

"She's not here, boy," she said disapprovingly holding tight to the cane that looked like was the only thing holding her upright.

"What do you mean?"

"I mean she's not here. She left. She's gone. Old Bob came to her door and told her she had four hours to get out. He said he wouldn't rent to no felon."

Abe blanched. Shit. This was one more thing piled on his head. "Where'd she go? Do you know?"

"Have no idea. We tried to talk to her, but she hasn't said more than three words to anyone since she got arrested. All her neighbors know she didn't do what those bitches said she did, but seems like no one else cares." She glared at Abe. "Besides, I'm not sure I'd tell you where she was, even if I knew."

Abe flinched but knew he deserved her ire. "I have to find her."

"Whatever." The lady turned around and hobbled back into the hall.

More determined than ever to find his love, Abe knew he'd have to rely on his SEAL contacts to help him. It might be unethical or even illegal, but he'd find her. He had to. He promised. Tex had helped him find her before, he'd do it again.

You promised.

He couldn't get Alabama's anguished words out of his head. They haunted him.

"YOU HAVE TO help me, Cookie," Abe pleaded with his teammate.

"I don't have to help you do shit."

Abe flinched, knowing he deserved that, and anything else Cookie had to say to him. He paced as Caroline, Cookie, and Wolf sat at a table and glared at him. Abe had called Cookie and Wolf and begged them to meet with him. They'd finally agreed. Caroline was also there when he'd shown up.

Abe knew he deserved the cold shoulder they were giving him, but he didn't care. He'd do whatever he had to do to find, and fix, what he'd done to Alabama.

After Cookie had talked with Abe and heard what

happened, he'd immediately called a lawyer and gotten the bond paid so Alabama could get out of jail. He'd gone to pick her up at the station and had been appalled at what he'd found.

He'd found Alabama, but not the Alabama they'd grown to love as a friend. She was broken. She didn't say more than a few words to Cookie or Caroline. She'd been locked behind bars for two long days. Cookie couldn't imagine what she'd been though. No, that wasn't right. He could all too well imagine it. Jail wasn't a good place to be, even if it was the local county lockup. He couldn't imagine shy, sweet Alabama in a place like that, and yet she had been. For three nights and two long days. If Abe had called Cookie sooner he could've gotten her out before she had to spend so long behind bars, but Abe had waited a few days before pulling his head out of his ass.

"We tried to get her to come home with us," Caroline spat at Christopher, "but she just shook her head sadly. She wouldn't even let us come up to her apartment with her. God, Christopher. I've never seen anyone broken like that before. I wanted to crush her up in a hug, but she wouldn't let any of us touch her. When we went back the next day to talk to her, to figure out what's going on, she was gone. All her stuff was there, but she was gone. A neighbor told us her landlord was going to throw all her stuff out since he'd evicted her and she hadn't taken it with her. So we packed it all up and put it in storage for her. What an asshole."

With every word Caroline spoke, Abe's heart hurt more and more. Wolf picked up where Caroline left off.

"I called my contact on the force and had a long talk with him. All off the record, of course. He told me he didn't believe Alabama had done it. The "witnesses" seemed too eager and knew just where to look on that damn cleaning cart to find the hidden pocket. He thought it seemed way too easy. He's been looking into it. Currently, he's going over the security tapes at Wolfe Realty to see what he can find. What do you want to bet he'll find Adelaide and her sidekick planting evidence?"

"God dammit!" Abe roared, punching the wall as hard as he could. He barely felt the pain in his knuckles. He turned until his back was against the wall and slid down until his ass touched the ground. Ignoring the blood trickling down his fist, he ground his fists into his eye sockets.

Caroline looked over at Wolf, who was frowning. She was still pissed at Christopher, but she couldn't stand witnessing his pain. She walked over to him and squatted down.

"We'll find her, Christopher."

When he looked up at her, Caroline was shocked to see tears in his eyes. She'd never seen her husband or any of the other SEALs cry. Ever. She couldn't imagine the pain Christopher was feeling.

"I've lost her. I don't deserve her. God, you don't even know."

Caroline sat down on the floor with her friend. "We'll find her."

Taking a deep breath Abe tried to get himself under control. "I'll find her. She won't want me anymore, but I'll make sure she's okay. I promised." His voice broke and he looked at Caroline. He remembered when she'd lain broken in a hospital bed. Remembered all she went through and how she was here with his friend and teammate today. Anguished, he repeated, whispering, "I promised, Ice, I *promised.*"

Caroline reached up and put her arms around the big SEAL. She couldn't do anything but hold him as he sobbed in her arms. She couldn't berate him anymore. Christopher was beating himself up more than any of them could. She had no idea where Alabama was, but she knew Christopher would do everything in his power to make sure she was safe, and that Adelaide and her minion would pay.

Chapter Seventeen

ALABAMA HUDDLED ON the cot in the homeless shelter. She was broke. All the money she'd saved up over the years was gone. She'd had to use some of it to pay the bond to get her out of jail. Hunter had paid it at first, but once she'd been able to get her hands on her own money, she emptied her savings account and given most of it to him.

He hadn't wanted to take it, but she'd refused to take it back. That had been eight days ago. Eight of the longest days of her life.

She had nowhere to go. No job. No money. No Christopher. *No.* She refused to allow herself to go down that mental road. She had to figure out what she was going to do. It was time to leave the west coast. Maybe she'd go to Texas…well, when she earned enough money for a bus ticket.

The only things she had with her were what she could fit into her one suitcase. She hadn't been able to take her little vase. She hadn't been able to take any of the belongings in her house that reminded her of better times. Hell, she hadn't wanted to take any of them at the time, but now…now she'd kill for one of her pillows that smelled like *him*.

It was harder than she'd ever imagined to let him go. Even though Christopher gutted her, she still loved him.

Alabama looked down at the one thousand two hundred and twenty three dollars in her hands. It was all the money she had left, but she couldn't keep it. She put it in the envelope sitting on the cot and reached for the pad of paper and pen lying nearby.

She penned the note, putting all her bitter feelings into her words. It didn't have to be this way, but she didn't know what she'd done to make Christopher dump her so brutally. Mama had been right all those years ago. Alabama was unlovable. If her own mama couldn't love her, no one could.

She finished the note and folded it carefully. It felt like her heart was breaking all over again. She stuffed it into the envelope with the money inside and wrote on the front.

For Christopher Powers, Navy SEAL.

She didn't know his address, but when she met with the lawyer Hunter had hired for her later that day, she'd give it to her to deliver. Once that was done, she'd feel better.

She had no idea what was going on with the case.

She knew she hadn't stolen anything, but Alabama had no idea if anyone would believe her. It would be her word, a janitor, against Adelaide's, who was a respected realtor in the area. It was hopeless.

Alabama knew she'd run before going back to jail. It'd been horrible. Oh, she hadn't been beaten up or raped or anything, but it was an awful place. She'd been watched at all times. The guards were broken down bitter men and women who had no empathy toward any of the inmates. The people behind bars with her, were just plain scary.

Alabama had stayed away from everyone, which wasn't hard considering it was just the local county jail. She'd taken meals in her cell and tried to figure out what to do. She didn't know how the justice system worked, so all she could do was wait.

She'd never been so glad to see Hunter in all her life. She wanted to cry, but she felt dead inside. She was nobody. Caroline had tried to talk to her, but Alabama shut her out too. She couldn't. Just couldn't. They were Christopher's friends. She didn't know why they were helping her. Hadn't Christopher told her what she did? She didn't ask. Just nodded at them when they dropped her off at her apartment and went inside without looking back.

Of course Bob had been waiting for her to kick her out. She knew he'd loved it. He stood at her door and watched her pack her meager belongings and demanded her key when she was done. She hadn't looked back, just walked out of the building and into the night.

Alabama stood up and grasped the handle of her suitcase. She couldn't leave it behind at the shelter while she met with her lawyer; if she did she might never see it again. A homeless shelter wasn't a place to leave anything unattended if you wanted to see it again when you returned. With the envelope in one hand and her suitcase in the other, she walked out of the room to meet with her lawyer in the common space downstairs. One way or another, Alabama hoped this nightmare would soon be over.

ABE LOOKED DOWN at the note and saw his hand was shaking. Actually shaking. He'd received a call from his commanding officer and he and Wolf had gone down to see him. Abe had been shocked when he'd been handed a thick envelope and that it had been delivered by Alabama's lawyer. He'd thanked his CO and he and Wolf had gone back to Wolf's office.

Now he sat looking at the envelope, knowing he wasn't going to like what was in it.

"Do you want me to open it?" Wolf asked seriously.

Abe shook his head and tore open the seal. Money spilled out onto his lap falling onto the floor as well. He looked up at Wolf then back down to the dreaded envelope. He ignored the bills and took out the plain piece of paper. It was a note from Alabama.

Abe read her words once then re-read them and read them a third time. He could almost feel the pain radiating from the words on the page.

Christopher.

Enclosed you'll find $1,223. I have no idea if this is exactly what I owe you, but it's as close as I can figure. I wouldn't want you to think I stole anything from you, so this is reimbursement for most of the things you did for me while we were…dating. Included in the $1,223 is: three pizzas delivered, four alcoholic drinks, two dinners, gas money for the times you picked me up from work and traveled to and from your place to mine, $157 for the flowers you gave me, and $400 or so for the groceries you bought when you made me dinners and lunches. I included some extra for things that didn't cost anything but your time, but time is money as they say. So for all the times you took me to work, held open my door, held my hand, and let me spend time with your friends and family, I've included reimbursement.

You might be thinking that I spent an awful lot of time remembering every single thing you did for me, and you'd be right. I only remember be-

cause you're the first man to do anything like that for me. Every single thing you did left its mark on me. I only wish I'd realized before now it was all payment for services rendered. I wish I'd known you were paying for me to sleep with you, I would've said no thanks.

I'm sorry I misunderstood. My fault. I hope I've returned everything. I wouldn't want to be accused of stealing from you.

—*Alabama*

Abe realized he'd been rubbing his chest while he'd been reading her letter. He knew he should be pissed at her. The Alpha man inside him wanted to punish her for throwing all of his gestures back in his face. On the surface, sending the money seemed like a petty thing to do, as she'd stated, but Abe knew Alabama well enough to know how much he'd hurt her. She was only trying to protect herself.

He leaned down and gathered up the money tucking it back into the envelope. He'd return it as soon as he could. In the meantime he'd have to figure out how he was going to help his woman.

"Help me, Wolf. Help me find her."

"You got it, Abe."

Chapter Eighteen

T HEY'D BEEN SEARCHING for Alabama for two days straight, with no luck. It was amazing how someone could just disappear. Abe would've been impressed, if he hadn't been so worried about her. Even Tex hadn't been able to dig up any reliable information to help find her. It was as if she'd disappeared off the face of the earth.

The team had split up around the city, each of them taking a different section. They hadn't found her, but they'd heard stories. The first time Abe had heard someone talking about Alabama, he'd been excited, thinking they were close, but it wasn't the case.

They'd gone into a small "mom and pop" grocery store with Alabama's picture asking the owners and workers if they'd seen her. They had. The clerk explained how she'd purchased five packets of those cheap packaged noodles college students were notorious for buying. Five. The total came to a dollar and forty two cents. She'd counted out the money from the change in her pocket. The clerk went on to tell them how he'd noticed her because after she'd made her purchase, he'd watched her walk across the street, kneel down next to one of the local homeless guys and give him one of the packets, and apparently the rest of the change she'd had in her hand.

So they'd left the store and tried to find the homeless guy. They hadn't found the exact person, but they'd talked to two other homeless women who'd said they'd met Alabama. They'd told Abe how sweet she'd been to them and how they'd let her stay with them on the street one night.

Abe was going out of his mind. He had over a thousand dollars of her money in his pocket and she was literally sleeping on the street and eating freeze dried-fucking-noodles. He wanted to howl his frustration. His woman shouldn't be living like that. She should be in his bed tucked in next to him. Safe. But he'd put her on the street. Him.

That night, after another day of searching with no luck, Wolf was fed up. "Jesus, we've had better luck finding terrorists inside third world countries! It's time to stop messing around. We need to trick her."

"No way," Abe immediately protested, not liking the thought of deceiving Alabama in any way.

Wolf immediately countered, "Do you want to find her, Abe? Or do you want her to spend another day and night on the street eating who knows what, meeting who knows what kind of people?"

Hell, when he put it that way, Abe was all about doing whatever Wolf wanted to do if it meant finding her. "What do you suggest?"

"We need to get her back with her lawyer. Alabama trusts her. We need to talk to her and get her to set up a meeting. Hell, she needs to meet with Alabama anyway. She has to get her to sign the papers acknowledging her freedom and the fact the case against her as been dropped. We have no idea if Alabama even knows Adelaide and Joni were arrested for making false statements. Those security tapes proved Alabama didn't steal anything and that Adelaide and Joni set her up from the start."

"Good idea."

"I'm not sure you should be there when we meet with her, Abe," Benny said.

"Oh hell no!" Abe said vehemently. "I have to be there. I started this and I'll finish it. I need her."

At the anguished tone in his friend's voice, Benny relented. "At least let us make sure she won't bolt before you can talk to her."

Reluctantly Abe nodded. He knew as well as the others did, if Alabama saw him first, that's exactly what she'd do, bolt. He deserved it, but he just hoped she'd give him a chance to grovel. "All right, set it up. Let's do this."

IT WAS TWO days before the lawyer could manage to get word to Alabama, and another day before the meeting was set up. The SEALs were impressed with the lawyer. As much as they hated it, she was able to find Alabama within forty eight hours.

Abe didn't care how she'd done it, just that he'd finally be able to see Alabama. He hadn't slept well since he'd realized what an ass he'd been. He fell asleep each night wondering if she was okay, and he'd wake up wondering the same thing each morning. His commanding officer was getting fed up with him *and* his team. They'd been worthless at work, and everyone knew something had to give. Abe didn't give a fuck though. Alabama came first in his life now. Before work, before his country, before everything.

Abe paced the hallway at the homeless shelter waiting for Wolf to give him the all clear. Alabama was supposed to meet with her lawyer in ten minutes. They all held their breaths hoping she'd actually show up.

The plan was to let the lawyer talk to Alabama first and break the news about the charges being dropped. Once she did that, Wolf and Dude would enter the room and let Alabama know they were there to talk to her. Once she settled from their arrival, Abe would go in. They had it all planned out, but no one knew what her reaction would be to it all.

ALABAMA WAS TIRED. She was dirty, sore, hungry, and perpetually scared out of her mind. Living on the streets was scary. It wasn't like the movies where everyone you met was nice and concerned about your welfare. People were on drugs and desperate and wouldn't hesitate to do whatever it took to get what they wanted. It wasn't all *Pretty Woman-esque* either. Alabama had been trying to avoid a local pimp for the last two nights. She knew if he could, he'd have her flat on her back working for him in no time.

She'd spent as many nights here in the shelter as she could, but when she'd heard Abe was looking for her, she'd bolted. She didn't want him to find her. It'd hurt too much. She was trying to figure out what to do, where to go, and how to get there.

When she'd heard her lawyer was needing to talk to her, she agreed to meet her today. Alabama couldn't wait to get the hell out of Riverton, but she had to make sure she was in the free and clear to leave. As much as she'd like to get out of town now, she knew she'd never make it far if she was wanted for skipping bond and leaving the state. So she'd stuck around.

The last time Alabama had talked to her lawyer, the woman had been convinced the charges would soon be dropped. She'd told Alabama there was a security camera in the Realty building. She'd point blank asked Alabama if she'd stolen anything. At Alabama's firm shake of the head, she'd simply nodded and said, "I didn't think so."

Alabama thought at the time it was pretty sad that a jaded lawyer had believed her with no questions asked, and Christopher, the man who'd told her he loved her, hadn't even given her a chance to explain. Alabama refused to let her mind go back down that road again. That part of her life was over. She was moving on. Of course it was easier said than done, but she was trying.

Alabama sat in the chair at the table in front of her lawyer. She'd left her suitcase near the door as she'd walked in. She felt dirty. Hell, she *was* dirty. She hadn't had a proper shower in days and her hair needed washing, badly. All she wanted to hear was that she was free to go, and she was out of here.

"Alabama, I've got great news," her lawyer gushed, not making her wait. "Those security tapes showed just what we thought they would. Adelaide and Joni planted the money on your cart and it's all on tape. I just got back from the District Attorney's office and all the charges against you have been dropped."

She paused, as if waiting for Alabama to leap up in joy or something.

Alabama just sat there. Whoopee. She was innocent. Big deal. She'd been innocent the entire time. She *was* glad at the decision, however, because it meant she was free to go. She tilted her head at her lawyer as if to ask,

"Are you finished?"

"I'm not done." She'd interpreted Alabama's non-verbal head tilt well enough. "There are some friends of yours here who've been looking for you. I agreed to let them join us in our meeting today."

At her words Alabama leaped to her feet. *No!* She didn't want to see anyone. She couldn't.

Just as the lawyer finished dropping her bomb, Matthew and Faulkner walked into the room. Their eyes took in everything about her with one glance. They saw her battered bag by the door. They saw her tired, haggard appearance. They saw the panic in her eyes.

"Sit down, Alabama," Wolf said sternly. "We want to talk to you."

Alabama didn't want to sit. She wanted to go. She glared at her lawyer. Why had she done this to her? Alabama had thought she'd liked her. Dammit.

Faulkner came over to her and firmly took hold of her arm and led her back to the seat she'd just vacated. He sat on one side of her while Matthew sat on the other side. Faulkner put one arm on the back of her chair and rested his other on his knee. Matthew just turned his chair toward her and put his elbows on his knees and leaned toward her.

"Are you okay, sweetheart?" Matthew asked softly. He wanted to touch this broken woman in front of him, but knew it wasn't his place. This was Abe's woman. He had to try to fix what Abe had done. Granted, Abe hadn't told them exactly what had happened when he'd gone to see Alabama at the station, but obviously whatever it was had broken Alabama. When she didn't answer him, Wolf looked up at Dude for a moment then tried again.

"Okay, dumb question. Of course you aren't all right. Hear me out, okay?" Not giving her a chance to agree or disagree he continued. "I've known Abe for most of his adult life. We were in BUD/S together. BUD/S is where we learned to be SEALs. I've saved his life and he's saved mine. Several times over. He's the one who got me to get my head out of my ass when I was ready to leave Caroline. He made me see I was being stupid and letting my head get in the way of my heart."

He stopped to reach over and take Alabama's hand in his. He noticed how much dirt there was under her nails and he winced. Jesus. It wasn't fair.

"He fucked up, Alabama."

At that, Alabama raised her head and looked at Matthew for the first time. She'd expected him to plead with her to forgive Christopher. To tell her what a great man he was. To take his side and tell her a sob story about what he'd been going through. She was ready for that. She could resist that. She wasn't ready for Matthew to so bluntly disparage his friend.

"Yeah, I know. You thought I'd come in here and tell you all about what a great guy he is and how you should take him back. Hell, I *do* think you should take him back, but I'd totally understand if you didn't. He made a huge mistake, Alabama. He knows it. You know it. We know it. But what you don't know is how much he regrets it."

When Alabama started shaking her head he squeezed her hand.

"I know. Regret doesn't change what happened to you. It doesn't change the fact you lost your home, that you spend three nights in jail. It doesn't change the fact you're currently homeless and penniless. It doesn't take away what he said to you, the hurt you feel. But it *could* change your future. What Abe won't tell you is the *real* story about how he came to be known as Abe. I will. If you'll listen…"

Alabama didn't want to. She really didn't want to. She wanted to hate Christopher. She wanted to despise him, but she couldn't. She loved him. Still. Even with what he'd said to her, she still loved him. She remembered every second they'd spent together. She remembered all the nights they'd spent loving each other.

Her heart was beating wildly in her chest. She was scared to death, Christopher could hurt her. He *had* hurt her. But if there was a one percent chance she'd get him back, she'd have to take it. She tilted her chin at Matthew to continue.

"Good girl. I'm so proud of you. You're the bravest woman I've ever met…well except for my Ice." He smiled so she'd know he was teasing her. Then he sobered and continued.

"When Abe was a little kid, he didn't know his father very well. The man would come to the house, then leave for months at a time. Abe never understood what was going on. That sort of thing would be confusing to any little kid. When he was eleven his dad left and never came home. His mom told him he'd died. It didn't really hurt Abe because he didn't know his dad that well. It wasn't until he was a teenager that he'd found out his mom had lied to him. She'd lied to protect him, but it still changed him fundamentally."

"His dad had a second family. Yup, a whole second family. He spent most of his time with that other family and not with Abe's. He'd come home every now and then to pretend, but then he'd be off again. He'd been killed when the brother of a *third* woman he'd set up and had kids with found out about his double, well triple life, and shot him. Abe wasn't upset with his mom. They're still close to this day, as you know. But the fact his father had lied to all of them, hell had lied to three different women and a total of eight kids, did something to him."

"Abe told me all of this one night when he was completely drunk, mind you. His dad's betrayal helped to formulate the man he is today. It's true he doesn't like it when people steal, but it's more the lies he can't abide. Here's where I try to explain what happened that day. Please know I'm not excusing his behavior in any way shape or form. But it might help you understand where his head was at."

Alabama didn't know if she wanted to hear it. This whole situation was crazy. She looked over at Faulkner who'd been sitting with his arm on the back of her chair the whole time. He simply nodded at her, encouraging her. Faulkner's jaw was tight and he looked pissed. Alabama didn't think it was at her, but the control that oozed out of every pore of Faulkner's body was daunting. Alabama turned back to Matthew.

He continued. "As you know, we'd just spent ten days in a third world country hellhole. I can't tell you what we were doing or why we were there, but as I'm sure you can guess, it wasn't to be diplomatic and "talk" to anyone. But while we were waiting to get home, Abe and I talked. This was the first mission since you guys had gotten together. He was missing you and worried about you. It drove him crazy because he'd never felt that way while on a mission before. He made mistakes. Nothing that would get him or us killed, but mistakes nevertheless. It was eating at him. We talked about how to handle it. I did the same thing on my first mission after getting together with Caroline. He was glad to be going home, to you. We hadn't had much sleep. In fact, I think he'd been awake for forty four hours or something like that. He went home straight to you, and the two of you probably didn't get much sleep that night either." Wolf smiled.

Alabama blushed. Wolf didn't comment on it, but squeezed her hand. "We'd just gone over the mission and discussed the mistakes that were made. He was feeling raw. He felt as if he'd let us all down. Then he heard about you, what you'd allegedly done. He was running on adrenaline and about three hours sleep in the last three days. He'd just learned how many mistakes he'd made because he'd been thinking about you and not about the job. He wasn't thinking straight, and he was hurting and embarrassed. He couldn't separate what his dad did in his mind, with what you were accused of. I know what he said to you was unforgiveable, Alabama. We're all pissed at him."

Alabama looked up at that. She was embarrassed all the guys knew what had happened, but she also suddenly felt bad for Christopher. These were his friends. She was a newcomer to their group, shouldn't they be on his side?

"Can you forgive him Alabama?"

Alabama looked down at her lap. If it hadn't happened to her she could've forgiven him in an instant. But it *had* happened to her.

Faulkner squeezed her shoulder without a word and got up from the chair next to her and left the room. Alabama looked over and saw that her lawyer had also left. She took a deep breath and looked at Matthew.

"I don't know." She whispered, answering Matthew honestly.

"Try, Alabama. Try. True love only comes along once in your life. That man loves you. He'd die for you. Trust me. I know." Matthew stood up, took her hands in his, kissed the back of both, ignoring the dirt, and left the room.

Alabama sat at the table thinking. What should she do now? She had no idea. She was a free woman, but still didn't have any money to her name. She looked toward her bag which she'd left by the door and gasped.

Christopher stood by the closed door silently watching her. How long had he been there? She watched as he slowly slid to the ground and finally came to a rest with his back against the door, his legs drawn up in front of him. He didn't say anything, but continued to stare at her intently.

Alabama stood up on shaky legs and crossed to the other side of the table. She wasn't scared of him physically, but putting distance between them was the only thing she could do at the moment to feel safe.

Abe cringed at her actions. He closed his eyes briefly then opened them again. "I deserve your mistrust. I do. I know it. But it kills me to see it. If it takes me the rest of my life I'll make it up to you, I swear."

Alabama didn't know what to do. One part of her wanted to leap out of her seat and rush to Christopher. The other part, the six year old who'd been locked in a closet over and over and had learned not to expect kindness, kept her standing in place and silent.

Abe sighed. Jesus. He hadn't let himself think about what he'd said to her that day in the interrogation room. She'd been scared to death and so relieved to see him, and he'd done the unthinkable. He'd thrown her love back in her face as if it meant nothing.

"If it matters, you should know I've ruined Adelaide."

When he said nothing more, Alabama raised an eyebrow at him.

"She might be facing charges for making that stuff up about you, but she'll definitely find out soon enough she shouldn't have messed with you."

"Christopher." Alabama's voice was tortured and rusty from lack of use. She never wanted him to do something like that for her. What if he got in trouble because of what he'd done? She didn't know *what* he'd done, but he obviously had the connections to do all sorts of things.

"Jesus, sweet." Abe choked out. He hated hearing how wobbly her voice was. She'd gone from speaking freely, to not talking at all in the space of a few weeks. And it was all his fault.

Alabama forced the tears back. She'd missed him calling her "sweet," but she wasn't ready to trust him again yet. She couldn't.

"I hate that you don't feel safe around me, Alabama. I know it's my own fault. I know it, but I hate it. I want you to feel safe. I'll do whatever it takes for you to have that again. I hope to Christ I can be in your life when it happens, but if not, I'll deal. It's more important for me to know you're safe, happy, and protected."

Now Alabama was crying.

Abe continued, forcing himself to stay seated and not rush across the room to hold her and tried to ignore her tears. Each one gutted him. "For what it's worth, I'm sorry. I was wrong. I was an asshole. I hurt you and I should've trusted you. It was inexcusable for me to say what I did. You know what I'm talking about."

She did. Alabama wasn't ready to forgive him, but his simple, straightforward apology went a long way. She didn't know many people who could come right out and admit they were wrong. Not to mention apologize for it in the same sentence.

"I'd do anything, and I mean *anything* to take it back, but I can't. All I can do is move forward and let you know it won't happen again. I know you won't believe that now, but I can say with one hundred and twenty percent certainty, I won't let you down again."

Abe took a deep breath. He knew Alabama wouldn't come running into his arms, but it still hurt to see her cowering behind the table on the other side of the room.

"Caroline is here to take you to her house. They got all your stuff that was left in your apartment and put it in storage when you were evicted. They went and got it all yesterday and moved you into their basement. You can stay there as long as you want. I talked to one of the Navy counselors on base and told her a little about you. She'd really like to talk to you…if you want. I left her information with Caroline. I'll stay away. You don't have to run to escape talking to me."

He took another breath and stood up slowly and gripped the doorknob to keep himself in place. "I know you hate me, sweet, and I don't blame you. But rest assured, I hate myself more. You didn't deserve this. You deserve someone better than me. You deserve someone who won't let you down. I hope like hell you can forgive me someday though."

Abe opened the door and gestured to Caroline that he was done. Wolf had allowed her to come with him and she'd been waiting in the hallway. She brushed by him, completely ignoring him, and rushed into the room to her friend.

Wolf stood off to the side in the hallway waiting for Abe as he exited the room.

"So?"

"She listened."

"And?"

"Don't know. It's up to you to convince her to stay. I'm sure she wants to bolt. I can't say I blame her. Take care of her, man."

"Oh, don't give me that shit, Abe. You aren't giving up on her. You can't. You wouldn't let me give up on Caroline; I won't let you give Alabama up."

"It's not up to me, Wolf. Ball's in her court. It's not the same as with you and Ice. I wouldn't blame her if she never said another word the rest of her life, that's how badly I screwed up. But I hope you and Caroline can get through to her. Get her to see that counselor."

Wolf put his hand on his friend's shoulder. "We'll do what we can. She'll come around. She loves you."

"And I love her. More than I ever thought I could ever love someone. But I hurt her. No, I devastated her. I'm not sure, if I was in her shoes, that I'd forgive me."

"She will, Abe. She will."

"I hope so. I sure hope so."

Chapter Nineteen

ALABAMA SLEPT FOR eighteen hours straight. Caroline had brought her to her house, given her a big hug, and left her alone in the basement apartment. It was just what Alabama needed. She needed some time alone to process all that had happened in the last month. She needed a safe place to hole up and get her balance back. She'd been through so many emotions, she was exhausted. She'd been scared, confused, hurt, sad, uncertain, and just plain tired.

Alabama took a long hot shower, scrubbing her skin raw, then, barely taking the time to dry herself off before putting on a T-shirt, collapsed into bed.

She'd woken up disorientated and confused, before remembering where she was. Her mouth felt like cotton and she knew if she breathed on anyone, she'd knock them over with her horrible breath.

Alabama groaned and rolled out of bed and staggered into the bathroom. After another long, hot shower Alabama felt more like herself. She'd forgotten she didn't have any clean clothes, all her clothes had been sitting in storage and needed to be washed, but when she walked out into the room she saw a pile of clothes on a chair in the corner. Caroline had obviously brought her some of her own things to wear.

Alabama pulled on the pair of sweat pants and the simple T-shirt, sans underwear. She debated with herself on whether she should go upstairs or not. Caroline had made it clear she was more than welcome, but Alabama wasn't sure she was ready to talk…or not talk. All it had taken was two little hurtful words from Christopher's mouth to put Alabama right back where she'd been when she'd met him. Wary and uncomfortable when talking to people. She reverted back to her old habits of keeping her mouth shut unless absolutely necessary.

She sighed. It'd be rude to stay shut up in the base-ment, besides she'd honestly missed Caroline. She'd become a good friend in the short time they'd known each other.

Alabama made her way up the stairs and opened the basement door and entered the kitchen. The smell of steaks grilling made her mouth water. She was suddenly starving.

Alabama didn't see anyone around, but knew Caro-line and Matthew had to be there somewhere. Instead of snooping around, she pulled out a chair from the kitchen table and sat.

Not too much later, Caroline came in from the other room.

"Alabama! You're awake!"

Alabama smiled shyly and nodded.

"I'm so glad you came up. Hungry?"

Again, Alabama nodded, a bit more enthusiastically.

"Okay, Matthew is grilling steaks. I swear he always makes enough meat for a hockey team. There's more than enough for you to have one too. Is that all right?"

Alabama forced herself to do more than just nod this time. "Yes, that sounds heavenly."

Caroline looked sad for a moment, then came toward Alabama and kneeled on the ground in front of her and engulfed her waist in a huge hug. Her head was buried in Alabama's lap and her voice was muffled when she spoke. "We were so worried. Thank God, we found you and you're okay."

Alabama was shocked. She had no idea Caroline had felt like that. Before she could respond, Caroline lifted her head, keeping her arms around Alabama and kept talking.

"Don't you ever do that again. If you're scared, or hurt, or *anything*...you call me. I'll come and we'll work it out...okay?"

Alabama didn't understand. "But, I hardly know you."

"Bull. We know each other, Alabama. I like you.

You're my friend. I'd like to think I'm your friend too. Let me put it this way, if I called you and said my car ran out of gas, would you help me?"

"Of course." Alabama didn't even have to think about it. Caroline had been nicer to her than almost anyone she could think of in her life before now.

"See? We're friends. That's what friends do for each other."

Alabama got it. For the first time she got it. She slowly wrapped her arms around Carline and belatedly returned her hug."

Caroline smiled and squeezed tight, then let go and stood up and held out her hand. "Come on; let's get some veggies together to go with Mr. Caveman's meat."

Alabama smiled and got up to help her friend.

LATER THAT NIGHT, Alabama sat on the bed in the basement with Caroline. After eating, Caroline had announced they'd have a slumber party. Alabama hadn't ever had a sleepover with anyone, and strangely enough, was looking forward to it.

It was silly really. She was thirty years old, but she needed someone to talk to. She wanted to talk about everything that had happened to her. She needed another opinion. She didn't trust her own feelings.

Matthew had been great throughout dinner. He hadn't brought up Christopher's name or talked about anything heavy. He'd talked and laughed with Caroline and tried to make Alabama feel as comfortable as he could.

Caroline changed clothes and wandered down the stairs later that night to join Alabama. Alabama had been sitting cross legged on her bed waiting. She could've watched television, but didn't really feel like paying attention to anything.

Caroline sat down next to Alabama on the bed and smiled.

"You look better. The sleep and food did you good."

Alabama made a conscious effort to talk to her friend. "I feel better. Thank you for everything. I mean it."

Caroline waved her thanks off. "Talk to me, Alabama. I know the basics of what happened from Matthew, and I saw how miserable Christopher looked, but I want to hear from you. What happened?"

"I honestly don't know, Caroline." Alabama told her. "I'd just had one of the best nights of my life, Christopher had come home safe from whatever scary mission he'd been on, and the next thing I knew, I was in an interrogation room waiting for him to come and get me out. But he didn't. He left me there."

Alabama took a deep breath. It was hard to talk about her childhood, but it'd be even harder to tell Caroline what Christopher had done.

"My mother abused me when I was little. She locked me in a closet and refused to let me out. She told me to shut up all the time, and if I spoke, at all, she'd beat me. I can't hear the words 'shut up' without remembering the terrifying nights I spent huddled on the bottom of a closet. Or feeling her hitting me."

"Oh, Alabama," Caroline said, emotion coating her words. "I'm so sorry."

Alabama knew she had to get the rest out before she lost her courage. "I thought Christopher was there for me. He wouldn't let me explain. He just kept ranting. Then when I tried one more time to talk to him, he told me to shut up." Ignoring Caroline's indrawn breath, Alabama continued. "He said the one thing that was guaranteed to rip my heart out and he left. He *left* me there. I spent three of the most terrifying nights of my life in jail, and believe me, that's saying something."

Caroline reached over and grasped Alabama's hand. "I've known Christopher for a while now, and while I can't imagine how you feel, how you *felt* hearing those words coming out of his mouth, it's obvious he's suffering."

When Alabama stiffened, Caroline continued quickly. "I know, you're suffering too. I'm not defending him, but he loves you, Alabama. He loves you so much. He sat in front of me and sobbed after hearing you'd had to spend the night in jail. The question is, did those two words kill your love for him?"

Alabama nodded immediately. Then changed her mind and shook her vigorously. Then she put her head in her hand and mumbled, "I don't know."

"You do," Caroline said with conviction.

"How do you know?"

"Look at what you're wearing, Alabama."

At the strange question, Alabama looked down at herself. She hadn't realized what she'd put on. She was wearing one of Christopher's T-shirts. She'd obviously grabbed it when she was packing up necessities in her apartment before she'd been evicted. One of Christopher's shirts had been folded up in her drawer and she'd packed it.

Alabama realized she'd worn it every chance she'd had. She felt closer to him when she was wearing it. For a while it had even still smelled like him.

Caroline pressed her point. "Could you see yourself walking away today, actually leaving Riverton and moving across the country, never to see him again?"

"Maybe it'd be best. I don't know if I can ever trust him again, nevertheless forgive him."

"Let me put it this way. What would you feel if he left on a mission and never came back? What if he was killed in action?"

Alabama didn't think. "Don't say that, Caroline! Jesus, don't *say* that sort of thing! You can't....he won't…" Tears came to her eyes.

"I'm sorry, Alabama. I had to make you *think*. He lives on the edge every day. *Every* time they leave the house there's a chance they might not come back. Don't you think I hate it too? I live with the worry every time Matthew leaves. But I trust him. I trust in his team. I trust in his love. You have to find a way to forgive him. You love him. Let that love guide you."

"But…"

"No buts, Alabama. I can guarantee you that Christopher will never, *ever*, say that to you again. He won't let anyone else say it either. He won't let anyone even *think* it. He learned his lesson. If you thought he was protective before, you haven't seen anything."

"What do you mean?" Alabama asked. Her mind was going in a million different directions. She loved Christopher. She was still beyond hurt by what he'd done, but she knew if she never saw him again, she'd be devastated.

"That man tore this city apart looking for you. Anytime anyone hinted he let you go, he lost it. Every time someone even *suggested* you might've been guilty, he lost it. That lawyer of yours? Hunter might have originally hired her, but Christopher harassed her every day trying to get information on you when they were trying to find you. He made sure she concentrated on your case and your case alone. And I don't know if he told you, but

Adelaide is going to wish she never messed with you too, I'll tell you that."

Alabama was stunned. She had no idea he'd been that concerned about her. She'd thought he'd dumped her, made a clean break. "He told me she'd wish she didn't mess with me, but not what that meant specifically. What'd he do to Adelaide?"

"Well, I don't know exactly, but Matthew told me some of it. They have a good friend out in Virginia named Tex He knows a lot of people and is really good with a computer. *Really* good. Adelaide's now broke. Her identity was 'stolen.' He told all her friends what she'd done and he had a talk with the Wolfe's. She doesn't have a job anymore and I'd be surprised if any of her friends stood by her."

"But that's...that's mean."

Caroline laughed harshly. "Alabama, that's not mean. What that bitch did to *you* was mean."

"But...Christopher's not like that. He protects people. He's a hero."

"Hon, she threatened you. She hurt you. *She* did that to you. Christopher is a trained killer, he could've done worse, and I have a feeling he would've if Matthew and the rest of his team hadn't reined him in."

At the shocked look in Alabama's eyes, Caroline continued in a softer voice. "He loves you. He loves you so much. He'd do anything for you, give you anything you want. He'll protect you with his life. You just have to forgive him and let him back in."

A lone tear finally dropped from Alabama's eye and spilled down her cheek. "I want to, but…"

"No, no buts. Give it a few days. Let everything sink in. You're safe here. You can be alone for as long as you need to be. You can stay here for as long as you want. I have the name of that counselor on the base if you want to talk to her as well. When you're ready, let me know, and I'll arrange for you guys to talk. Okay?"

"Okay. Caroline?"

"Yes?"

"I've never had a best friend before. Hell, I've never even had a close friend before. But I'd like to call you my friend."

"Oh girl…If you didn't, I'd have to bitch slap you."

The two women laughed together breaking the tension. Finally, being tired, they drew the covers back on the bed and climbed in. The heavy talk done, they giggled and gossiped for a long while before finally drifting off to sleep.

Chapter Twenty

WHEN ALABAMA WOKE up, Caroline was gone. Alabama didn't blame her. If Christopher had been nearby, she probably would've climbed into his bed too. She had a lot to think about. She wanted to forgive Christopher, she still loved him, but she had no idea *how.*

She might still love him, but she wasn't sure she trusted Christopher anymore. He'd broken her trust in the most brutal way possible. He'd left her to face the false accusations by herself, not to mention leaving her to spend time in jail.

Alabama sighed. As Caroline had told her last night, she wanted to think about things for a few days. She hadn't completely decided if she was leaving or staying in Riverton, but she was pretty sure she was staying. She wanted to get to know Caroline better and besides, Christopher and his team were stationed near here.

Alabama got out of bed and took a shower. She lovingly folded and put Christopher's shirt under her pillow for when she got ready for bed again. She wandered upstairs, hoping to see Caroline again.

Caroline wasn't around when she made her way to the kitchen, but Matthew was. He told Alabama Caroline had to work that day, she was making headway into a new chemical process. Matthew admitted easily he had no clue what it was, but Caroline wanted him to tell Alabama she'd be home for dinner.

"What is it Alabama? I can tell you're thinking heavily about something. Spit it out."

"It's just...I don't understand why you guys are letting me stay here. Don't get me wrong, I'm thankful, and I really like Caroline, but I don't get it."

"Abe has saved my life more than once. He even saved my woman's life. Caroline told me a little about what you went through when you were a kid and I already knew what Abe said to you. It was unacceptable and hurtful, we all know that and we're all more than pissed at Abe because of it. But the thing is, you're still his. Being his, makes you, by default, mine; and Mozart's, and Cookie's, and Benny's and Dude's. We made a vow to protect each other with our lives, and that extends to our families."

"But..."

"No buts," Matthew said interrupting her. "You're ours to protect, and that means protecting you against hurtful words too, no matter who they come from.

Until you're ready to talk to Abe, you're under my protection. No one will get near you without my say-so. When I'm not here, one of the team will be. We're giving you the time you need to work through what happened in your mind. If at the end of your thinking, you decide you don't want to stay, we'll respect your decision. But fair warning, we'll still probably try to convince you otherwise."

Alabama just stood there staring at Matthew. He couldn't be serious. "But, you guys have to work."

"Yeah, we do, but we've worked out a rotation and got it okayed by our commander. Anywhere you want to go, anything you want to do, you've got one of us to help you do it."

Alabama just shook her head. "You guys are crazy."

Wolf smiled. "Get used to it."

THE NEXT FEW days were surreal for Alabama. Every morning when she made her way upstairs she found a different member of Christopher's team waiting for her. One morning Hunter was standing at the stove flipping pancakes. He'd calmly asked her what she wanted to drink. Another morning Kason was sitting at the table eating doughnuts from a huge box. The third morning Alabama thought she'd finally been left alone, only to find Faulkner sitting outside the house in his car. When she'd left the house to take a walk he'd gotten out of his car and walked with her.

Matthew was right. They were there, looking out for her, simply because they thought she belonged to Christopher.

Finally, after a week had passed since she moved into Caroline and Matthew's basement, she thought she was ready. She'd gone over and over what had happened in her mind. She didn't *think* she'd been at fault, except maybe she could've talked faster and *made* Christopher listen to her. But the bottom line was that she still loved him. She wanted to see him; she wanted to hear what he had to say.

It was Saturday. Caroline had picked up some cute clothes for her yesterday on her way home from work. She apologized to Alabama for not thinking about it earlier and swore they'd soon spend all day at the mall making sure Alabama had everything she needed.

Alabama took advantage of the cute clothes she now owned and put on a pair of jeans with a tank top. The tank top wasn't sexy per se, but it showed more than Alabama was used to showing. She knew she was stressing over seeing Christopher again, but she couldn't help it.

When she entered the kitchen, Caroline and Matthew were sitting on a chair at the table. Caroline was in his lap and they were so busy kissing each other they didn't even know she'd entered the room until she cleared her throat loudly.

Alabama laughed at the blush that spread across Caroline's face. She watched as Matthew's hand eased out from under her shirt and grasped her around the waist. He wouldn't let her jump up off his lap though.

"Good morning, Alabama," he said in his low rumbly voice. "Did you sleep well?"

Alabama simply nodded. She didn't want to go through the niceties this morning. She got right to the point. "I'm ready."

The couple knew exactly what she was talking about.

"Awesome." Caroline exclaimed quietly.

"Thank God," Matthew said fervently. He leaned forward with Caroline on his lap and reached into his back pocket for his phone. Alabama watched as he swiped the phone to turn it on and pushed some buttons, obviously sending a text message. In just a moment, he put the phone on the table in front of him and said, "He'll be here in a few."

"What?" Oh my God. Already? Even though Alabama had said she was ready, now that Christopher was actually going to be here, she was panicking.

"Yeah, he's been spending every night in the driveway, in his car."

Alabama thought her head was going to explode.

She felt like a parrot repeating everything she heard. "What? He's been spending every night in the driveway, in his car?"

Matthew chuckled and settled Caroline deeper into his chest, her head tucked under his chin. "Yeah, he wanted to watch over you himself. We tried to tell him you were safe and nothing would happen to you in our basement, but he insisted."

"That's…insane."

"No, hon," Caroline finally chimed in, "that's love."

Alabama didn't have time to say anything because the doorbell pealed throughout the house. She looked at Matthew and Caroline. They hadn't moved.

"Are you going to get it?" She asked them.

Matthew laughed. "We all know who it is, Alabama. Go and put him out of his misery…and yours."

Alabama took a deep breath and slowly walked toward the door. She knew she'd said she was ready, but now she wasn't so sure.

She slowly opened the door. She put a hand on her chest. Just the sight of Christopher was enough to bring back the pain she'd felt when he'd told her to shut up in the police station.

Abe stood in front of Alabama with his hands in his pockets. He was nervous as hell. He'd screwed up so badly, but all he wanted was a chance to talk to her, to apologize.

"Hey."

"Hey."

"Thank you for agreeing to see me."

Alabama just nodded. She suddenly felt tongue tied again. She knew he wouldn't disparage her again, but it was still hard for her to talk to him as she'd once done.

"Will you come with me today? Will you trust me enough to keep you safe for the day?"

Alabama nodded automatically. It wasn't that she didn't trust him…exactly. Okay, that wasn't completely true. She knew he'd keep her safe from physical danger; it was her emotional safety she was more concerned about.

Abe let out a long breath, as if he'd been holding it waiting for her answer. "Do you need to get anything before we go?"

Alabama nodded. "I'll meet you at your car?" She didn't know why, but she wanted to talk to Caroline and Matthew again before she left.

"Okay, sweet, I'll wait for you out here. Take your time." He took a step back. He seemed to understand her uncertainties.

Alabama shut the door and went back into the kitchen. Her friends hadn't moved. "I'm going out."

"Good. Remember what we talked about, Alabama," Caroline told her seriously. "Give him a chance."

"Can I…" She paused, biting her lip.

"What is it, Alabama? Can you what?" Wolf sat up straighter as he asked.

"Can I call you to come get me if I need to?"

Wolf felt Caroline about to answer and squeezed her hip hard. She kept silent and he slowly put her aside so he could stand up. He kissed Caroline lightly, then walked over to Alabama.

Wolf reached out for her, watching for signs of her pulling away. She didn't and he enfolded her into his embrace. "Of course you can, Alabama. I don't care where you are, when it is, if it's today, or ten years from now. You need me, or Caroline, or anyone on the team, you call. We'll come running. Okay? You're not alone. You have all of us now. We aren't letting you go no matter how this turns out today. You'll be fine, but if you need us, we're here. Just call and we'll come. Okay?"

Alabama nodded. Wolf pulled back and kissed her on the forehead. "Now, go on. Try to enjoy the day. Get the heavy stuff over with so you can enjoy being with your man again. Make him grovel, but in the end, take him back."

Alabama gathered what little strength she felt she had around her, and pulled away. "Okay, thanks. Have a good day, guys."

She grabbed her little purse and went back toward the door and Christopher.

Wolf snatched up his phone and quickly tapped out a text to Abe before Alabama had even made it to the front door.

Alabama opened the door and stepped out, watching as Christopher put his phone into his back pocket before he started toward her.

ABE FELT SICK inside. He'd read the text from Wolf. Jesus. She'd gone back inside to ask if they'd come and get her if she asked. He wanted to kick his own ass. He'd done this to her. She didn't trust him and he couldn't blame her. Today was the first step at getting her trust back. Abe didn't know what he'd do if he didn't earn it, but he'd spend the rest of his life trying, if only she'd let him.

"You ready, sweet?" The endearment slipped out without any thought on his part.

Alabama nodded and allowed Christopher to open the passenger door of his car. He helped her in and held out the seatbelt for her. Once she was secured, Abe closed her door and walked around to the driver's side.

Starting up the car, he turned and looked at Alabama. She was beautiful. He'd missed her, but it was his own fault. He'd done a lot of things he regretted in his life, but hurting Alabama was at the top.

"I thought we'd go downtown, have some lunch, then maybe walk along the beach. Does that sound okay?" He didn't want to do anything she'd be uncomfortable with.

"Yes." Alabama answered softly, but at least she'd answered.

Abe found a parking spot downtown and they entered the small trendy café down by the water. He asked for a table outside, hoping being unconfined would help her relax. He even let her have the seat against the wall.

Alabama knew how badly Christopher was trying to make her feel comfortable the second he offered the seat against the wall to her. She recalled the conversation they'd had the first time he'd taken her out for coffee about sitting against the wall so he could see the room.

She shook her head and took the other seat instead. He wouldn't admit it, but she could see the relief in his eyes. Christopher hadn't wanted to take the other seat, but he would've if she'd wanted him to.

They ordered drinks and sandwiches and sat in awkward silence for a couple of minutes. Finally, after their drinks were delivered, Abe broke the silence.

"I know I've already apologized, but I hope you'll let me do it again. I'm sorry. Jesus, I'm so sorry."

When Alabama didn't say anything, but remained looking at him with sad eyes, he continued.

"I have nothing to say to defend myself. I hadn't had a lot of sleep, I heard what you'd been accused of and I immediately thought about my asshole of a father.

If I'd only stopped to think for half a second I would've known the truth. But I didn't. I rushed to the station and said shitty things to you. I didn't believe it."

At her look of disbelief he swore. "I didn't, sweet, I swear to God. I was confused and hurting, and I took it out on you."

When he stopped talking and just looked at her, Alabama knew she had to tell him of her experiences. She looked at the tabletop instead of at him while she spoke. "I thought you were there to help me. I was so scared. I asked for them to call you and I was so relieved when you walked in the door. Then you said...that...I couldn't believe it. I didn't understand."

Abe made a choking noise, but she didn't look up. "Every night when I was in that cell I was scared to death. Some of the other inmates said some...things...to me. I didn't know if I was going to get out of there or not. I couldn't eat. I didn't sleep more than twenty minutes at a time. Throughout it all, all I could think of, all I could see was your face, all I could hear were your words, as you came into that interrogation room."

Alabama risked a look up at the man who'd hurt her so badly. He looked anguished. She continued quickly wanting to get it all out in the open. "I didn't take a shower while I was in there because I was afraid to take my clothes off. When Bob was yelling at me calling me a felon, I didn't know what to do. All I could do was grab some things and get out. You hurt me Christopher. No, you devastated me."

Alabama continued quickly, before Christopher could say anything. "I was ready to leave. I wanted to get away from here, away from the hurt I'd felt." She paused, then looked up and stared Christopher in the eyes. She was amazed to see they were swimming in tears. "But then Caroline asked me a simple question and I knew I had to see you again. I had to give you another chance."

Abe blew out the breath he'd been holding. He'd never hurt as badly as he had in the last few minutes listening to Alabama talk about what she'd been through, what *he* had put her through. He'd been shot, stabbed, beaten, and starved, but nothing had hurt as badly as her words.

"What'd she ask you, sweet?" Abe asked softly, dreading her answer, but wanting to hear it nevertheless.

"She asked how I'd feel if you left on a mission and never came back."

The air between them cackled. Neither broke eye contact when the waiter brought their lunches and set down the plates on the table.

Abe waited for her to continue.

"I knew then that I still loved you. You hurt me, but God, I love you, Christopher."

Abe pushed his chair back from the table and took a step toward Alabama. He knelt down on the floor and lightly put his hands on her knees. Alabama was shocked. She hadn't expected him to get on the floor. She could feel the heat from his hands seeping through her jeans and she soaked it in as if she was a plant that had been in the darkness for months.

"I don't deserve you, Alabama. Lord knows I don't, but I love you too. I don't want you to go. I want to woo you." At her half laugh, half snort, he grinned, then sobered up again. "Yeah, it sounds silly, but I want to show you that you can trust me again. I want to show you how important you are to me. I know SEALs aren't known to have lasting relationships, but I'll do everything in my power to make sure you know you come first in my life. Yes, I might have to fly off at the last minute for an assignment, but if push comes to shove, you'll come first. I'll go AWOL or tell my commander to take me off the mission list if I have to. You're it for me, sweet. I'll spend the rest of my life earning your trust back."

"I've never come first to anyone before," was Alabama's timid response.

Abe wasn't expecting it. He didn't know what he expected, but it wasn't that. He picked up one of her hands and kissed the back of it. He wanted nothing more than to haul her into his arms and kiss her deeply, but he knew he hadn't earned her back yet. "You're the most important person in my life, Alabama."

They grinned at each other and Abe slowly got up off the ground. He kept hold of Alabama's hand and went back to his seat. They ate lunch and both were glad of the decreased tension in the air between them.

After lunch, Abe took her to the beach as he'd promised. They'd wandered up and down the sand laughing at the antics of the seagulls that were constantly looking for food.

The trip back to Caroline and Wolf's house was made in comfortable silence. Abe wanted to reach out and hold Alabama's hand, but knew it was too soon. It could've been weird, knowing they loved each other, remembering the times they'd spend loving each other in bed, feeling the distance between them now, but Abe was happy for whatever she'd give him.

Now that Abe knew Alabama still loved him, he knew he had a chance. He'd go as slowly as she needed him to. All he wanted was her trust. Love was one thing, but trust was what made a relationship solid.

He pulled up to Wolf's house and shut off the car's engine. Abe turned to Alabama. "Thank you, sweet. I don't deserve you. I know I told you this before, but I'll say it once more. I'll never give you a reason to distrust me again. You need me, I'm there. No matter what. I don't care if someone tells me you've killed someone. I'll never doubt you, and I'll always give you a chance to explain, whatever the situation is. I'll never walk out on you again. I know you don't trust me now, but you will. I swear."

Alabama gave him a sad smile. "I hope so, Christopher. I need you. I need your trust. I don't think I can get through the rest of my life without it."

"Come on, sweet. Let's get you inside. I'm sure you're tired."

They walked up to the porch and stood in front of the door. "I feel like I'm on a first date," Alabama tried to joke.

"In a way we are." Abe leaned toward her and lightly kissed her lips. He then moved to her nose, then her forehead, before stepping back.

Alabama couldn't stand it anymore. She looked up at the man she loved with every fiber of her being and stepped into him. He immediately put his arms around her and clasped her to him. Alabama snuggled into his body, wrapping her own arms around his waist. They stayed like that for a couple of minutes, neither wanting to let the other go.

Finally Alabama straightened and pulled away. "I'll see you later?"

Abe brushed his knuckles down her cheek. "Of course, sweet."

"Go home, Christopher. You don't need to sleep in

your car. I'm okay. I'll talk to you tomorrow, okay?"

He smiled. She was so cute. "I'll talk to you tomorrow." He ignored her request. He'd sleep outside Matthew's house until she was back in his arms, and bed, for good. He'd promised to put her first, to look out for her, and dammit, that's what he was going to do.

Alabama just shook her head at him. She reached for the door handle and turned it. With one last look at him, she disappeared into the house.

Abe breathed in a sigh of relief. He'd been so scared she wouldn't forgive him, that she wouldn't love him anymore. He was thankful Alabama was so forgiving. He wasn't sure he'd be the same way if he was in her shoes, but he wasn't looking a gift horse in the mouth.

He turned to head back to his car and his bed for the night. He had a "wooing" to plan. He couldn't wait.

Chapter Twenty-One

THE NEXT FEW weeks went by fairly quickly. Christopher had been true to his word and had been doing his best to woo Alabama. He'd come over to the house at least twice a week to spend time with her and Caroline and Matthew, and they'd also spent almost every weekend together. He'd even encouraged her to spend time with his mom and sisters. The Saturday they'd gone shopping was one of the most fun times Alabama had ever had.

His family was hysterical. They'd been horrified at what had happened to her. She appreciated they hadn't defended what Christopher had done; in fact, they'd all cussed him out. Alicia even took her phone out to call him and tell him what an ass he'd been.

Luckily Alabama was able to calm her down. They'd talked through everything that had happened over lunch. There were still swear words thrown out, but there were also tears. Alabama hadn't realized how much she needed to be able to talk through what happened with someone that wasn't directly involved.

The three Powers ladies had commiserated with her and supported her. After their initial shock, they'd also supported Christopher. They didn't tell Alabama anything she didn't already know, but they'd told stories about Christopher when he was little. Alabama got a better idea of how he'd made himself into the man he was today, and how much the actions of his father had affected him.

Christopher came over that night and they'd had another long talk. Alabama told him all about how his family had reacted and while he winced only once, all he said was, "I'm glad you were able to talk to them, sweet."

Alabama had just started working again. She didn't go back to Wolfe's, and none of her friends blamed her. Greg and Stacey had come to see her to apologize and beg her to come back, but Alabama knew she wouldn't be able to. They'd let her down. They'd believed Adelaide and Joni over her, without asking any questions.

Christopher's commander had given her a reference and used his contacts to get her a cleaning job with a local office building. It held several different businesses. The best thing about the job was that she didn't have to work evenings anymore. While she preferred cleaning when others weren't around, no one really spoke to her as she went about her cleaning duties.

She'd been embarrassed to tell Christopher, after all she was only a janitor, but when he'd heard, he was thrilled for her. He told her there was no shame in what she did for a living. She was still a bit embarrassed, after all he had such a larger-than-life job and she didn't, but she changed the subject when he'd tried to talk to her about it again.

Alabama's life was settling down. She had good friends for the first time in her life, and she loved hanging out with Christopher and his teammates. She'd gotten to a point where she was ready to get back to where they'd been before, but she had no idea how to get there with him. It wasn't as if she could come out and say, "Hey, I'm ready to sleep with you again."

ABE WAITED OUTSIDE Wolf's house. He'd worked really hard to get Alabama to trust him again. It seemed as if he was making progress, but he didn't want to rush her.

Alabama opened the door and his breath caught in his throat. Damn, she was so beautiful. She wasn't wearing anything overtly sexy. In fact, he knew she'd probably be embarrassed if he told her how hot she actually looked.

She was wearing a pair of shorts that came down to her knees, and her usual V-neck T-shirt, today it was pink, and a pair of flip flops with a giant pink flower on them. Her toes were painted a bright pink as well. Obviously she liked the color and had gone all out to accessorize on her shopping trip with his sisters and mom.

"Hey, sweet, you look beautiful."

As if on cue, she blushed.

Alabama didn't say anything, but held the door open for him to enter the house. Abe had never heard her say so much to anyone at one time as she had to him when she'd explained how she'd been affected by his actions when they'd been at lunch. She'd never be comfortable speaking in public or large crowds, but Abe knew she was getting more and more relaxed when speaking with him or to others when he was around.

Abe leaned in and kissed her on the side of her mouth when he got close enough. He took the door out of her hands and shut it.

"Where's Wolf and Caroline?" Abe knew they weren't going to be there, Wolf had given him a head's up that day at work.

"They went out to dinner and then they were going to go to a movie afterward."

Abe put his hand on the small of her back and steered her toward the kitchen. "So, it's just you and me tonight huh?"

Alabama blushed again. Jesus, she had to stop. It wasn't as if he'd announced he was going to throw her on the sofa and make love to her all night long…not that she'd complain. They'd already explored and tasted every inch of each other's bodies, it shouldn't be embarrassing to think about making love with him. Alabama simply nodded, affirming they'd be alone most of the night.

Entering the kitchen, Abe saw a pot of water boiling on the stove. He chuckled. "What're you making me tonight?" It was a running joke between the two of them now. She'd never be a gourmet cook, but she could make a mean pasta dish.

"Just spaghetti."

"Aw, sweet, it's never 'just' spaghetti. I love your spaghetti."

Alabama rolled her eyes at him. He laughed and put his arms around her waist while she stirred the noodles.

"Don't you know? I don't care what you make us to eat. I'm just happy to spend time with you. Anything you make, I'll eat with a smile on my face."

Alabama smiled weakly up at him. She knew she wasn't the best cook, but she'd kept herself alive this long, they wouldn't starve.

They talked while the sauce bubbled on the stove and they chopped vegetables for the salad. When the noodles were ready, he drained them while Alabama got the dressing out of the fridge. They served themselves and set their plates on the small table in the kitchen.

They ate the simple, yet delicious, meal in comfortable silence.

After putting the dishes in the dishwasher they sat on the sofa. Alabama wanted to bring Christopher downstairs to her little apartment, but she had no idea how to bring it up, so she stayed silent.

Abe put in a movie and they watched it for about an hour. Just as Bruce Willis was about to blow something else up, the doorbell rang. Alabama looked at Christopher in surprise.

Seeing that Alabama wasn't expecting anyone, Abe told her, "Stay put sweet, I'll see who it is."

Abe opened the front door and saw two police officers standing there. They were slightly overweight and had their hands on their belts, as if ready to defend themselves. Abe hadn't heard Alabama come up behind him, but he heard her indrawn breath.

"Oh my God," she exclaimed softly, "Is it Matthew and Caroline? Are they all right?"

Abe had been thinking the same thing, but the brown haired cop quickly reassured them.

"No, no, it's nothing like that. Are you Alabama Ford Smith?" He peered at Alabama suspiciously.

Abe put his hand around Alabama's waist and pulled her to his side and partially behind him as she said simply and cautiously, "Yes."

"You'll need to come with us ma'am. We have some

questions we need to ask you at the station."

Abe felt Alabama go stock still. He could feel the tension course throughout her body. Oh hell no. "What's this about?" He demanded, not so gently.

"There's been a reported burglary at the building down on Main and Third. We have some information that Ms. Smith works there and has been arrested in the past for theft. We only need to ask her some questions."

"Fuck no." The answer was swift and growled with menace.

Alabama looked up at Christopher. She couldn't control her breathing. Her breaths were coming out fast and hard. It was happening again. Oh God...

"You have no idea what you're talking about. If you'd read those reports a bit more carefully you'd have known she was falsely accused. You'd have known she has one of the best lawyers this city has ever seen."

"Sir, all we want to do is ask her some questions." The shorter of the two police officers was getting visibly irritated.

"She didn't do it."

"You don't know what it is..."

Abe interrupted the man. "No, because whatever you think she did, you're wrong. She didn't do it. She didn't steal dick."

Alabama kept her eyes on Christopher's face. She couldn't look at the officers. She was shaking hard enough as it was—she couldn't look at their uniforms, it would bring back too many memories. Listening to Christopher defend her from…hell, she had no idea what it was he was defending her from, but it was as if a warm blanket straight from the dryer had been wrapped around her. Christopher was defending her. He was pissed on her behalf. This was what she'd expected all those weeks ago. *This* was the man she'd fallen in love with.

"You want to ask her questions? Fine, we'll come down in the morning, with her lawyer. And, if you don't have probable cause to question her, you'll be wishing you hadn't bothered us."

"We can't just…"

Abe wasn't letting them get a full sentence out. "You can, and you will. Is she under arrest?" At the negative response, he continued, "Then, we'll see you in the morning at the precinct."

Abe slammed the door in the officer's faces and turned Alabama into his body. He pulled her until she was belly to belly with him. He could feel her trembling. It infuriated him. How dare they come here and scare her. How *dare* they assume she had anything to do with whatever was missing. Abe was pissed, but he tried to stay calm. He needed to stay calm for Alabama.

The warmth of Christopher's body felt so good. He'd wrapped his arms around her—one arm around her waist pulling her into his body and the other against her back. He placed his hand on the back of her head, pushing it into his chest. Without moving, she mumbled, "Can you even do that?"

"Hell yes. And I just did. They had no evidence. They had no reason to come over here this late at night. They only wanted to scare you. Assholes."

They stood there for a few more minutes, then Abe said through clenched teeth. He was nowhere near calm. "I gotta call Wolf and the rest of the team, sweet. Let me tell them what's going on, they'll take care of it and will get your lawyer to meet us at the station tomorrow."

"You didn't let them take me."

"What, sweet? I couldn't hear you." Abe leaned his head down until his ear was near her mouth.

"You didn't let them take me," Alabama repeated.

Abe took the hand that had been on her head and put it under her chin. He tipped her head up until she had no choice but to look him in the eyes. "I told you I'd never doubt you again. I love you. I'll protect you with my life if I have to. You don't *ever* have to deal with anything by yourself ever again."

Alabama's breath hitched. He *had* said that, but she hadn't believed it until right then. All she could do was nod. She stood on her tiptoes to brush her lips against his.

At the first touch of her lips Abe swooped in. The

kiss wasn't sweet, it wasn't gentle. It was a claiming. Abe claimed his woman again. She was his and he wasn't letting her go.

Alabama let Christopher take the lead; she'd follow him wherever he wanted to take her. She was his.

ALABAMA SNUGGLED INTO Christopher's side. It'd been a long night. Christopher hadn't let go of Alabama throughout the evening. He'd kept her close to his side, touching her, soothing her, calming her. After the intense kiss they'd shared, he'd called Matthew. He and Caroline had rushed home and set up a sort of command post on their dining room table.

Soon the house was overflowing with testosterone. The entire team had banded together. It was the most amazing show of support Alabama had ever seen in her life. Personally, she thought it was a bit of overkill, especially since she'd spent the day with Matthew and Caroline and hadn't even been alone all day, so she had a pretty good alibi, but she'd never say anything to the men who were discussing their next steps.

Christopher had called her lawyer and she'd agreed to meet them at the station in the morning. She was going to call and see what had happened before they met up so they'd have a head's up as to what was going on.

Every one of the men had told her she had their support before they'd left. When Hunter had hugged her tight and told her if she ever wanted to leave Abe, he'd be right there ready to snatch her up, she finally lost it.

At the sight of her tears, Abe had almost gone ballistic. It wasn't until he realized she was crying tears of happiness at all the support she'd been shown, that he finally calmed down.

Now they were lying on her bed in the basement. He was wearing jeans and his button up shirt and she'd changed into the T-shirt of his she'd been sleeping in for the last few weeks. He didn't say a word about it, only smiled possessively when he'd seen her. Christopher was on his back with his arm around her and she was on her side. Her head was resting on his chest and one of her legs was thrown over one of his. She was surrounded by him, and she loved it.

"I love you."

Christopher's arm tightened around her. Alabama could feel the muscles in his bicep twitch on her back. It was the first time she'd said it outright to him since the day she'd been arrested.

"Sweet," his voice was tortured. "I don't deserve you. You're way too good for me, but I can't let you go. I won't."

"You don't have to, Christopher. I'm yours for as

long as you want me."

He rolled toward her until she was on her back look-ing up into his eyes. They were intense. "I'll always want you. You're mine."

His head dipped and for the second time that night he kissed her with all the dominance he'd been holding back for the last few weeks.

Alabama's hands went to his head and clenched his hair as he ravaged her mouth. Finally he pulled back, just enough to look into her eyes.

"Don't worry about tomorrow, sweet. Trust me to take care of it, of you."

Alabama couldn't believe he'd stopped. She was ready for him to make love to her again. "I know you will…now shut up and kiss me."

She loved seeing the smile creep over his face.

"Whatever you want. Whatever you want."

Epilogue

CAROLINE AND ALABAMA sat on the couch and tried to pay attention to the movie that was playing. Neither was doing a very good job of it. Finally Caroline shut off the television.

"When were they supposed to land again?" Alabama was more than ready to see Christopher again.

The team had been called out on a mission to Mexico. They weren't able to tell them where exactly they were going or what they were doing, but both Caroline and Alabama knew whatever it was, it was dangerous.

Each mission had been easier and easier for Alabama to take, but she knew it'd never be *easy*. Every time Christopher walked out of the house, whether it was for a mission or for a simple trip to the grocery store, she worried.

Christopher had been steadfast in his support of her. He'd taken care of the "misunderstanding" the night they'd gotten back together. The police officers had even apologized for bothering her that night. Alabama knew Christopher was behind that, but he'd never admitted it.

Alabama had quit the cleaning job she'd had, with Christopher's urging and support, and decided to go back to school. She wasn't sure what she wanted to do, but for now she was taking general education classes. She had time to decide later. She hadn't wanted to not work, but Christopher had convinced her after one long night in bed, that she'd be better off concentrating solely on her studies.

She'd gotten closer to his friends and teammates, and she worried almost as much about them as she did about Christopher, almost.

Caroline watched as Alabama paced. Caroline missed Matthew just as much as Alabama missed Christopher, but she'd been with him longer, so she'd had more experience in the agony of waiting for him to return from a mission.

"They'll be home as soon as they can, Alabama."

"I know, I just miss him."

Finally after another hour passed, the women heard a truck in the driveway. They both raced to the front door and out into the yard.

Alabama had eyes only for Christopher. He met her in front of the truck and held her to him in a hard, possessive embrace. As usual, she burst into tears.

"Jesus, sweet. I'm fine. Wolf's fine. Everyone's fine."

"I know," Alabama said between sniffs, "I'm just so happy you're home. I missed you!"

Christopher picked her up, carrying her toward the door. Every time they came home from a mission Matthew invited them to stay in her old basement bedroom. They'd always agreed because driving to their townhouse seemed as if it would just take too long.

"I missed you too, sweet."

Alabama inhaled Christopher's scent as he carried her into the house. She didn't bother to look up at Caroline and Matthew; she knew they'd be doing the same thing she was.

As Christopher carried her down the basement stairs she quickly asked, knowing if she didn't, she'd be way too preoccupied to ask for the next few hours. "Everyone okay?"

Abe loved how she was always concerned for his teammates. They were like brothers to him and it showed just how sweet Alabama was that she always asked. "Yeah, everyone's okay. We got the girls out, they're gonna be okay."

"Girls?"

"Well, women. I'm not supposed to talk about it, but in nutshell this woman had been kidnapped a few days ago. We went in and found her easily, but there was another woman there too...she'd been there for a couple of months. Cookie stayed back in Texas with

Benny and Dude to help her…acclimate."

"God, I love you, Christopher. You know that right?"

"I do, sweet. I love you right back."

"I'm proud of what you do. Those women are so lucky you and your team do what you do."

"It's missions like that that make our job easier. Even though it was tough, it's always nice to be able to save people." Abe stopped talking. Alabama was obviously done rehashing his mission. She was unbuttoning his shirt and kissing every inch of his chest as she bared it. He grinned to himself, he'd let her have her fun for a bit, he knew soon it'd be his turn.

He'd make contact with Cookie and check on the woman…later. Much later.

Look for the next book in the
SEAL of Protection Series:
Protecting Fiona.

Discover other titles by Susan Stoker

SEAL of Protection Series

Protecting Caroline

Protecting Alabama

Protecting Fiona

Marrying Caroline (novella)

Protecting Summer

Protecting Cheyenne

Protecting Jessyka

Protecting Julie (novella)

Protecting Melody

Protecting the Future

Delta Force Heroes Series

Rescuing Rayne

Assisting Aimee (loosely related to DF)

Rescuing Emily

Rescuing Harley

Rescuing Kassie (TBA)

Rescuing Casey (TBA)

Rescuing Wendy (TBA)

Rescuing Mary (TBA)

Badge of Honor: Texas Heroes Series

Justice for Mackenzie
Justice for Mickie
Justice for Corrie
Justice for Laine (novella)
Shelter for Elizabeth
Justice for Boone
Shelter for Adeline (TBA)
Justice for Sidney (TBA)
Shelter for Blythe (TBA)
Justice for Milena (TBA)
Shelter for Sophie (TBA)
Justice for Kinley (TBA)
Shelter for Promise (TBA)
Shelter for Koren (TBA)
Shelter for Penelope (TBA)

Beyond Reality Series

Outback Hearts
Flaming Hearts
Frozen Hearts

Writing as Annie George

Stepbrother Virgin (erotic novella)

Connect with Susan Online

Susan's Facebook Profile and Page:
www.facebook.com/authorsstoker
www.facebook.com/authorsusanstoker

Follow Susan on Twitter:
www.twitter.com/Susan_Stoker

Find Susan's Books on Goodreads:
www.goodreads.com/SusanStoker

Email: Susan@StokerAces.com

Website: www.StokerAces.com

To sign up for Susan's Newsletter go to:
http://bit.ly/SusanStokerNewsletter

Or text: STOKER to 24587 for text alerts on your
mobile device

About the Author

New York Times, USA Today, and *Wall Street Journal* Bestselling Author Susan Stoker has a heart as big as the state of Texas, where she lives, but this all-American girl has also spent the last fourteen years living in Missouri, California, Colorado, and Indiana. She's married to a retired Army man who now gets to follow *her* around the country.

She debuted her first series in 2014 and quickly followed that up with the SEAL of Protection Series, which solidified her love of writing and creating stories readers can get lost in.

If you enjoyed this book, or any book, please consider leaving a review. It's appreciated by authors more than you'll know.

Printed in Great Britain
by Amazon